# SCARE ME

# SCARE ME

## K. R. Alexander

Scholastic Inc.

ISBN 978-1-338-33881-2

10 9 8 7 6 5                    21 22 23

Printed in the U.S.A.   40
First printing 2019

Book design by Baily Crawford

For those who love
to be scared

# O

**Nothing scares me.**

That's why I'm the best at what I do—making haunted houses. My friends and I, we're called the Bloody Banshees, and every year we make it a point to outdo ourselves and scare the entire town of Happy Hills in our yearly haunted house competition.

We've created some of the scariest rooms this town has ever seen. Labyrinths filled with terrifying beasts. Chambers filled with horrific old dolls and cracked mirrors that reflect back ghosts. A circus tent complete with contorted clowns and roaring zombie lions.

But this year, I know we have to do more. Ever since our rivals, the Monster Mashers, cheated and stole our title last year, I've been dreaming up something even more terrifying than all our old scares combined. This year, my team and I will create something so horrifying, even the bravest adult will fear going inside. We'll create something that *might* even scare me. It will have to be completely, utterly horrifying. And I think I have the perfect plan.

Nothing will get in our way.

Nothing human, at least . . .

# 1

"Ewww, I have fake blood on my shirt!"

I glance over to Julie, who—sure enough—has bright red corn syrup dripping down from the pocket of her T-shirt.

Tanesha breaks into laughter.

"That was me," she says. "I put a blood capsule in your pocket. Don't worry—it will wash out."

Julie glowers over at her, but Julie's anger never lasts very long. Almost immediately, she starts laughing.

"Good one, Tanesha, but just remember—"

"I don't get mad, I get even," both Tanesha and I

say. And then we all start giggling. It's Julie's favorite phrase. But I'm pretty certain that she's never actually tried to get even.

Which is good, because Tanesha is a master prankster. If Julie tried to pull one over on her, I don't think it would end well.

Still giggling, we continue carrying our crates of scary props to the big old mansion in front of us. Three stories tall, with fading blue paint, huge windows, and a yard the size of a football field, Corvidon Manor is our town's largest and oldest home. Most of the year, it's a history museum, where people can look at old photographs of our town or talk to Mr. Evans, the proprietor, who gives free tours. I've been inside a few times for school field trips. From November to September, it's pretty boring.

Then October arrives.

For the month of October, Corvidon Manor is our playground. Every Halloween, Happy Hills holds a fund-raiser for our animal shelter. Four teams of kids each design a creepy experience for the mansion, one per floor, including the basement. The one with the scariest floor gets a year's supply of pizza and ice cream from Jolly Jerry's Pizzeria.

For the other teams, it's just a fun way to raise money. For me, it's a life calling. Someday, I want to build real haunted houses or work in movies. I take this seriously.

Which is why, when I see Patricia's mom's sports car rounding the corner, a sick acid roils in my gut. She and her team beat us last year. And they didn't win fair.

"Come on, Kevin," Tanesha says, noticing my stare. "We're going to win this year. Don't let her psych you out."

I nod glumly.

"Bloody Banshees forever," Julie says hopefully. Our little slogan.

"Bloody Banshees forever," Tanesha and I repeat.

I stare up at the house as we reach the wraparound patio. In the summer, this place is green and filled with birds and a gurgling fountain. But it's like the moment October hits, the house itself knows it's game time. The trees in the yard have already turned a deep red orange. The fountain no longer gurgles and instead sits heavy with fallen leaves and wary toads. And maybe it's my imagination, but the closer we get to the house, the colder it seems to become.

As if the house knows it's time to get scary.

As if it, too, is excited.

Our feet creak on the wooden front steps.

Behind us, a murder of crows startles from a tree, flying off in a flutter of angry caws and black wings and orange leaves.

Julie shivers.

"Do you think that's a good sign?" she asks quietly.

I smile.

"Definitely. I think it's a sign that this year is going to be the scariest yet."

# 2

Mr. Evans holds open the front door for us as we lug our first load of decorations inside. Today is for scouting out the space—we've got paper and pens to plot the layout and decide what exactly we need. Tomorrow, my dads will bring it all to the manor in their truck. That way we'll only have the necessities and can get right to work. I kind of have this down to a science.

"Thank you, Mr. Evans," I say as we pass by.

"Of course, children. Do you already have something scary dreamed up for this year?"

I smile to my friends. "Oh, we've had this figured out since last Thanksgiving."

Mr. Evans chuckles as he guides us down the hall. He honestly looks like he's as old as the manor, if not older. He has wispy white hair and round wire-framed glasses and always wears suspenders. He looks old and frail, but something about him says he will live forever. "I expect nothing less from the Bloody Banshees. You were *so close* to winning last year. I bet you'll take the gold this time around. If you'd follow me? I know you know where to go, but I'll show you to the basement."

The long hallway is carpeted in plush, well-treaded crimson, and the faded floral wallpaper has turned yellow over the years. The air in here distinctly smells of lemon cleaner, mothballs, and dust. It's a smell I've started associating with Halloween. Antique curios and bookshelves line the hall, and above them are photos from our town's past: farmers in the field, a gathering at town hall, that sort of thing. One of them catches my eye—it's a photo from *ages* ago, and the woman in white stares down at us unhappily.

It must be a trick of the light, but I swear she scowls at me.

Despite the sleepy warmth of the hall, shivers wash over my skin. But instead of creeping me out, it makes me smile. I mean, I *know* the picture didn't move. The fact that my imagination is already geared up for scare mode has me excited. I love that feeling. This is going to be a *great* year.

The feeling of excitement and chills intensifies as we get closer to the basement. We pass by an open room that is currently an explosion of boxes and costumes. The Masked Mummies have already started setting up their creepy fun house. I nod at them and smile (since my hands are holding a box of animatronic plastic skeletons), and they wave back. Except for my rivalry with the Monster Mashers, I try to stay friendly with the competition.

Mr. Evans opens the door to the basement for us. Our feet creak on the wooden steps as we walk down, the air dropping ten degrees the moment we pass the door.

My smile widens.

The basement is already creepy. Concrete floors

and flickering lights and low-hanging air ducts and metal support pillars scattered about. It's damp and dusty and smells like a crypt.

Which is why it will make the perfect graveyard.

I can already picture it—I'll put papier-mâché around the support pillars and turn them into trees and hang moss and cobwebs from the ducts, and we'll throw in some creepy lighting so everything looks moonlit. Then we'll gather some leaves to throw over the ground and—

"You're doing it again," Tanesha says.

I snap out of it and look at her.

"What?"

"Looking around like you're about to make this a whole heck of a lot more work than it needs to be."

Despite her words, she's grinning. Tanesha loves building haunted houses almost as much as I do.

"What can I say? I'm inspired."

The door clicks behind us. I didn't even hear Mr. Evans say goodbye, I was so caught up in my daydreams.

"You're always inspired," Julie says.

"Just because my friends are so inspiring," I reply.

Julie and Tanesha both roll their eyes.

"What do we do first, boss?" Julie asks.

I set my box down by the steps. The basement is lit by a few bare bulbs dangling from the ceiling. Creepy, but too industrial for the ambience we're going for. For a split second, I consider changing our theme to some sort of abandoned-warehouse-torture-chamber, but then my eyes snare on something in the back corner.

"Dang it," I mutter, walking toward it. "They were supposed to clean before we got here."

Because there, lurking in the shadows, is a pile of what I'm assuming is old junk. Maybe posters or furniture from upstairs.

Julie and Tanesha follow at my side as we near.

When my eyes adjust and I see what the shape is, I shudder.

Facing the wall is a large mannequin wearing a wedding dress and veil. Julie inhales sharply.

"That's just creepy," she whispers. "I don't want to touch it."

"Me neither," Tanesha whispers. "Maybe we should get Mr. Evans."

"It's just a mannequin," I say. I look to Tanesha

skeptically. She's normally the brave one of my friends. "And why are you whispering?"

She shrugs. She doesn't take her eyes off the mannequin.

We step toward it slowly, and for some reason I can't make my heart stop beating frantically in my chest. The mannequin is tall and slender, made of pure white porcelain. Its face is completely smooth, featureless, which makes it even more eerie behind its lace veil. The dress it wears is beautiful and ornate, though definitely old—the hems are frayed and ragged, and it looks dusty and tan rather than pure white. Something about it just seems . . . sad.

There's something at the base. A little placard resting on the stand the mannequin poses on. For some reason, it makes me pause. Maybe this isn't just a leftover. Maybe this was some sort of display. One that's been hidden from the public for a while.

I crouch down and try to make out the words, but I can barely read them in the gloom. There are newspapers pasted to the sign. I can make out the headlines **TERRIBLE TRAGEDY** and **MISSING BRIDE**. I peer in closer, squint, and try to make out the words.

## Local Bride Drowns Herself in Lake.
## Mourning Family Creates Counterfeit.

A loud thud echoes from upstairs, and I flinch up to standing. I knock right into the mannequin bride as I do so.

"Careful!" Julie yelps.

I reach out and grab the mannequin as fast as I can, but it's too late. Although I catch it by the arm, her head keeps falling, toppling off her shoulders. It seems to fall in slow motion. I watch it, heart paused in my throat, a sense of dread in my gut. It can't fall. It can't fall—

Her head crashes to the ground, exploding in a million tiny shards of porcelain.

Julie yelps. Even Tanesha makes a startled noise.

I stand there, still holding the rest of the mannequin up, and stare at the remains of her head on the concrete. I don't know why, but the sight almost makes me sick. I glance over to the placard, to the photo I can barely make out and the headlines burned into my thoughts. **TRAGEDY TRAGEDY TRAGEDY.** I try to shake the dread from my bones. It's way too early on to get creeped out, and we have a lot of work to do.

"Dang it," I mutter, making sure the rest of the bride is stable when I let go. "Now we have to clean *this* up."

"I hope we don't have to pay for it," Tanesha says.

"It feels like we already have," Julie whispers.

# 3

Tanesha runs upstairs to grab a broom and comes back with Mr. Evans. He takes one look at the mannequin before shuddering himself. His eyebrows furrow with confusion.

"What?" I ask. I stand beside him while my friends start unpacking. They're more than happy to be far away from the mannequin in her dress, but I'm intrigued. It creeps both of them out, so there has to be something to it.

"Oh, nothing," Mr. Evans says. He starts to sweep up the shards of her head into a dustbin. For a moment, I worry that he's not going to say any more.

Then he continues. "It's just that I thought our people got everything out of here. Packed it all up in a big truck and moved it into storage. I don't know how they could have missed this. Honestly, I forgot we'd even held on to this thing. Such a sad, sad story."

More chills wash over me.

"You mean this wasn't supposed to be here?" I ask. I keep my voice low, so my friends can't hear.

"The whole basement was meant to be cleared out for you. Sorry about this."

"It's okay," I say, an idea worming its way through my heart. "What did you say you were going to do with the rest of it?"

Mr. Evans looks at me with an eyebrow raised.

"Why?"

"No reason," I say. "Just wondering."

I try to sound disinterested, but Mr. Evans seems to see right through it.

"She's just going to go into the broom closet upstairs until we find out where she's supposed to be. She is *not* meant to be a part of this contest. As you know, the rules forbid you from using the objects that belong to the house. You must provide your own scares!"

I nod and ask him how admissions were this summer, hoping to make him think I don't care about the creepy mannequin or where he's going to hide it. The truth is, I can't get the mannequin out of my mind. It feels important. More important than just some old trash left in the basement. I want to know its story. Its "terrible tragedy" of a story. Something shifts on the mannequin and I glance over to see a large, furry black spider crawl out from the bride's neck before scurrying into her dress. I shudder. Not much scares me, but that doesn't mean I like creepy crawlies.

Which makes me think . . .

I wanted to create something that might scare even me, and when I look at the broken bride, I think I may have found the answer. The question is: Am I willing to risk it?

Last year, Patricia broke the rules and got away with it.

Why can't I this year?

# 4

Mr. Evans moves the bride back upstairs after he's cleaned up her shattered head.

I can't help but watch him go—just seeing the bride tugs at my chest, and not in a good way. I mean, it creeps me out, so I guess it's a good thing. It's just weird; I'm not used to being creeped out.

"What was it even doing here?" Julie asks. Her voice wavers.

I shrug and kneel down, picking up the placard at the mannequin's base. I read the small article aloud. This one isn't from a newspaper, but seems to be some sort of museum piece.

*Missing Bride Found—Local Tragedy Unfolds. In late winter of 1941, the body of Miss Anna Corvidon was found in the frozen Lake Charm. Earlier that winter, her fiancé, Mr. Colin James, had died in the war. Their wedding had originally been set for a few days after he was deployed. He never returned. Although originally thought an accident, authorities believed the grief-stricken Anna was so devastated by the loss of her fiancé that she drowned herself in the frozen lake. She was found the next day by her family. Miss Corvidon's family was never able to recover. Shortly after her funeral, they dressed a store mannequin in her gown, preserving her memory for the fiancé, who would never lead her down the aisle. The mannequin stood in their care up until their deaths; then it was bequeathed to the historical society. Some believe the mannequin is haunted, and caretakers have reported strange sounds or shadows whenever the mannequin is installed.*

I swallow and look to my friends, my gut sinking and pulse racing.

"That's terrible," Julie says.

"Yeah," Tanesha replies. "The poor girl." She looks at me and smacks me on the arm. "And you had to go and break her head!"

"I didn't mean to," I say, rubbing my arm. She hits hard.

"Well, hopefully Mr. Evans can fix it and she can, I don't know, rest in peace."

I swallow. I have a feeling neither of them would like it if they knew what I was thinking. Not just because they are very much against breaking the rules, but because it's clear they feel bad for the girl.

But . . . it was just a dress on a mannequin, right? Not the girl herself. And it's not like I was planning on stealing it or anything. Just borrowing it for our display.

A shadow twitches in the corner of the basement. My heart freezes. Was that—? No. Strange.

I thought there was a woman in the corner.

More thudding upstairs brings me back to the task at hand.

"Come on, we have a lot of work to get done tonight."

My friends nod, and together they go sort plastic spiders from the spiderwebs while I begin mapping out the basement. It's one large open space, with a low ceiling supported by concrete and steel beams and a bare concrete floor. *The swamp can go here in this corner, but we're going to need a few extension cables for the fog machine and air pump. We can line up the skeletons over here. Dang it! I think the caskets are too tall for the ceiling. We'll have to prop them at an angle. How in the world am I going to get the lights installed on those beams?*

"ACK!" Julie yelps.

I jolt around in time to see her leap into the air. My heart immediately starts racing—did she see something, too?

"What?" Tancsha asks.

Julie stares wide-eyed at the fake webs.

"That spider isn't plastic."

Sure enough, a large black spider scuttles from the webbing, vanishing into the shadows of the basement. Just watching it makes my skin crawl. Is it the same one from the bride? It almost makes me feel like we're being watched.

Cold trickles down the back of my neck, making my hairs stand on end.

It definitely feels like we're being watched.

I glance over to the placard still in the corner, to the place where I thought I saw a shadowy figure. There's nothing there. And yet, I could swear that's where the feeling of eyes is coming from.

"There better not be more of those," Tanesha says. "I hate spiders."

"Probably not," I say. "Besides, we don't have any poisonous spiders here. That was probably just a daddy longlegs."

"Right," Julie says. Then she mumbles under her breath, "It was way too big to be a daddy longlegs."

Julie doesn't return to the spiderwebs. She starts pulling out the Styrofoam tombstones instead.

Before we can really get back to business, the door opens and a new set of footsteps tromps down the stairs. I think I know who it is before I even turn around. When I do look, my stomach sinks further and anger simmers in my veins.

"Patricia," Julie says.

"What are you doing down here?" I ask my nemesis.

Everyone seems to think Patricia is innocent.

Probably because she looks like a stereotypical angel—long blond hair, blue eyes, and skin so pale I don't think she ever goes outside. Her voice, too, is high-pitched and sweet, and she always wears frilly old-fashioned clothes—which honestly just makes her look creepy, in my opinion. Like she thinks she was born in another century. Adults think she's darling, and that means she can get away with a ton of bad things.

Like what she did to us last year.

Just the thought brings my anger from a simmer to a boil.

"I heard a scream from all the way up in the attic," Patricia says with her cherubic smile. "So I thought I'd come down and see what you'd done to scare yourselves."

"I stubbed my toe," I say quickly. "Nothing scary."

"Really?" Patricia asks. "You scream like a girl."

I shrug. My best friends are girls—the insult means nothing to me.

But Patricia isn't even paying attention to my reaction. She's already stepping past me and staring over my shoulder at the stuff we have unpacked. I move to block her, but obviously it doesn't work. We have too much out in the open.

I should have locked the door.

"Huh," she says.

"You're not supposed to be down here," I say. "You know the rules. No snooping."

"I'm not snooping," she says, still surveying our décor. Both Julie and Tanesha stare at her with open animosity. They step to my sides to help block her view.

She goes on. "I was just concerned. What was Mr. Evans carrying up? I heard you broke something."

"None of your business," I say. I have to force myself not to grind my teeth or look toward the mannequin's placard. The last thing I need is for her to seek the mannequin out herself.

"Maybe you should go," Tanesha says. "I'd hate to have you disqualified for breaking the rules so early in the game."

Patricia steps back and gives us her most innocent smile.

"I'm just a concerned friend. Wanting to make sure everyone here is okay." The smile drops, and the real Patricia shows herself. "You're going to need to up your game if that's all you've got. I was kind of hoping it would be a real competition this year." She sends an unimpressed glance up to our spiderwebs before leveling an even less impressed glance back at us. "And frankly, so far, I'm not convinced." Then she smiles again, sweetly, like she didn't just insult our entire project, before turning on her heel and prancing up the stairs.

I growl under my breath when the door clicks shut behind her.

"Don't let her get to you," Tanesha says. She puts her hand on my arm. "She's just trying to distract us."

"It's working," I grumble. I glance back to the foam tombstones and fake cobwebs. And I think of my brief conversation with Mr. Evans, the idea that had seemed risky but now seems like the only way forward. We need more than some killer props and design—we need a story. A *terrifying* story, one that makes people connect with our exhibit. I'd been waiting for the missing piece, and the bride is it. My anger fades into resolve. "Come on," I say. "We have a lot to do before going home."

In the back of my mind, I promise myself again to do whatever it takes to make this the scariest year ever. Even if it means going behind Mr. Evans's back. Patricia thinks we need to up our game? I'll up our game. I'll prove that she shouldn't underestimate us.

No matter what, we're going to have a terrifying graveyard.

Ghost bride and all.

# 5

Julie and Tanesha both head home a little bit before I do.

I hang back in the basement while waiting for my parents. We've gotten as much done as we can—the basement is fully mapped out and I have a long list of things to pack and bring with me tomorrow, so we should be able to get everything installed right away. Then we have one more day to get everything dressed and figure out the small details. The three of us work really quickly together, which is good since we don't have much time. This is going to be the most ambitious year yet.

I slowly detangle the strands of purple lights, still thinking about what Patricia said and wondering if maybe she's right. Maybe we *don't* have a chance. Her parents and friends have a ton of money, so she's able to get the best practical effects.

It's not fair.

I glance over to the animatronic skeletons lined up against the wall. They stare at me with empty eyes. And empty heads, too, as we forgot the batteries to bring them to life. They're new. I bought them on sale at the end of Halloween last year, and when I did, I was sure that they would be the key to winning this year. They can record messages and parrot them back to the audience whenever someone walks by. It's just a shame they don't move as well. I was going to hide a few behind tombstones and others within the gates of a mausoleum, and when people walked by, the skeletons would laugh and scare everyone half to death.

But now, when I look at them, I can only think that they look fake. Cheap. You can see the LEDs in their eye sockets and the wires in their joints. Maybe we didn't lose last year just because of Patricia. Maybe we lost because my team can't afford scarier things.

I sigh and try to fight down the sadness. Without my friends around, it's hard.

"This is your year, Kevin," I say to myself, trying to psych myself up. "And someday, you're going to make special effects for big movies and haunted houses and you'll be famous."

It's the same thing I've told myself every night for the last month, to pump myself up.

"This is your year, Kevin," comes a creepy electronic voice.

I startle and look to the skeletons. One of them has glowing green eyes, and its mouth moves jerkily as it talks. Its teeth look oddly rotten, and I swear that mud cakes its bones. It leans forward, just a little, which should be impossible, and turns its head

ever

so

slowly

to face me.

Its broken teeth and twisted mouth turn up into a sneer.

"This is your year, Kevin," it says again.

"What in the world?" I whisper. My heart races in my chest. "I thought you didn't have batteries?" Maybe one of my dads put batteries in to test it out?

"This is your year, Kevin," it repeats. Its voice is less mechanical this time. More feminine. Creepier. Chills race down my back as I take a step closer.

"How are you—?"

"This is your *fear*, Kevin," the skeleton says. I stop a foot away from it; I don't want to get too close. I don't want to consider the impossible—that it might reach out and grab me. It must be malfunctioning. Something wrong with the mic or—

**"You wouldn't let me rest, Kevin. And now, neither will you."**

The lights in the skeleton's eyes blink out.

Silence returns to the basement.

Silence, if you don't count the thud of my heart.

Silence, if you don't count the screaming in my head.

And when I reach out and pick up the skeleton, I

realize something that—for the first time in my life—makes me truly afraid.

The battery case really is empty.

The skeleton came to life on its own.

**I don't want to go to sleep.**

After my dads picked me up, we went home and sorted through all my old decorations in the basement. It took an hour. And then I had to do homework. And even though it's late and I'm tired and in bed, I don't want to close my eyes.

Because no matter what I do, I can't get the talking skeleton out of my head.

I'm not *scared*.

I don't get scared.

I'm just . . . confused.

Yeah. That's it.

It has to have been Patricia's doing. Maybe she managed to sneak in a wireless speaker or something. Maybe she switched out the skeletons when I went on a bathroom break. There has to be some logical explanation of what happened, and I'll bet anything that Patricia is the force behind it.

After all, that's one of the reasons I love haunted houses: Everything inside is explainable and safe. Every single scare is created by a normal person like me, and once you realize that, it's not so scary. It's just cool to see how they did it. Which means I need to figure out how Patricia did it, because it was a creepy effect, and I'm sure it would scare someone who could actually, you know, get scared.

So yeah, I'm not awake because I'm freaked out. I'm awake because I want to know how Patricia pulled it off.

Soon, it's almost midnight, and I'm no more tired than I was when I went to bed at eight. My dads are asleep and the house is quiet, and as I lie there, staring at the ceiling, my thoughts drift from Patricia and the skeleton to the ghostly bride. If I'm going to use her in the display, I need to know her story. I need to make her *real*.

I roll over and grab my phone from the nightstand. Maybe if I start reading about her, I'll tire myself out so I can sleep. I squint against the brightness of the screen and start to research.

It doesn't take much to learn about her. All I do is type in *Happy Hills* and *ghost bride* and a dozen articles show up. Each is creepier than the last.

I scroll through articles by the local newspaper, as well as blog posts by fans of the story. The headlines are almost as scary as the content: **MOURNING FAMILY CREATES NIGHTMARE. GHOST BRIDE LIVES AGAIN.**

One article in particular makes me pause: **UNABLE TO MOVE ON, FAMILY BRINGS DEAD TO LIFE.** I read through, and with every word goose bumps creep up over my skin.

Turns out, Anna's family didn't just create the mannequin bride to remember their daughter. They created it to *replace* their daughter. When she died, they were completely devastated. They say her mother snapped.

My blood runs cold as I read on.

Anna had been buried in her wedding dress. But her mother dug her up and removed it, putting it on the mannequin because she couldn't let her daughter go. The police tried to get involved, but it sounds like Anna's parents were big deals. They actually built Corvidon Manor and half the town. No charges were ever pressed, and the whole thing was forgotten. Except . . .

I scroll down further, and there are photos scattered throughout the text. Old black-and-white pictures. A man and woman in the dining room. And there, propped awkwardly in the corner, is a mannequin dressed in white. The next shows a huge bed, the woman sitting on its edge and the mannequin bride tucked in with the covers to its chin. The next shows the mannequin bride in the manor's window, Anna's mother at its side, waving.

I blink. My breath catches.

Did it—?

No. It couldn't have. I keep scrolling.

There's no way the bride turned to look at me.

I must be more tired than I thought. But that doesn't stop the chills from crawling all over my skin, nor does it calm my sudden desire to turn on all the lights in the room.

I feel like I'm being watched again.

From the corner.

From the shadows.

*Get ahold of yourself. It's just your imagination.*

It doesn't make me feel any better.

I read through the end of the article, which just talks about how the mannequin bride stayed in the manor after the parents died and the whole place became part of the historical society. Nothing super interesting. Then I turn off my phone.

Darkness settles around me like hands pressing against my chest. Once more, I want to turn all my lights on, but that's not like me. I don't get scared. There's a logical reason for my fear—I read an article that triggered an emotional response, and in the darkness, my imagination is allowed to go haywire.

It doesn't matter how much I tell myself that.

The chills don't go away.

The feeling of being watched doesn't fade.

It doesn't matter that I know it's all in my head.

As sleep swims in, I know I hear a woman crying.

# 7

**My nightmare begins like this.**

I stand in the hall of a mansion. The walls tower above me, the ceiling so far up I can't even see it in the shadows. Great drapes billow down the sides like splashes of blood, and everywhere I turn, in every corner, along every wall, is a mannequin. Or part of a mannequin. Smooth-faced porcelain mannequins or fully detailed ones with eyebrows and lips and glass eyes, of all shapes and colors and sizes. They stand facing the walls, or upside down in enormous brass flower pots, or illuminated on bureaus. Everything is silent. So silent, I can hear myself breathing, can hear the blood in my veins.

I take a step forward. My foot squishes deep into the carpet. But

it doesn't feel like carpet.

It feels like something alive,

or mostly alive.

The moment I take another step, I catch something from the corner of my eye and freeze.

The mannequin nearest to me moved.

I look over to it. It's one of the more detailed mannequins, with blank eyes and red lips. It doesn't look any different, but I *swear* it moved. I swear it moved to stare at me.

I swear it wasn't smiling before.

Another step. I have to get out of here. My pulse races in my ears and now I'm not so certain that I only hear my breathing.

I think I hear other inhalations.

I think I hear the mannequins breathing.

Another step, and I *know* the mannequin I pass turns. Its head cocked to the side, whiplash fast, watching me run. Because I *am* running now. Running down the squishy hallway as the drapes billow with hidden breezes and the mannequins jerk and turn to watch me flee. As they jerk and follow me.

As they run, too.

And suddenly I am running down a hall that stretches toward infinity, and as I run my feet start sinking into the carpet and I can barely take a step, can barely lift my legs from the mud-like floor, but the mannequins behind me are close now, so close, and I can't let them get to me. Can't let their cold porcelain fingers reach me.

Something claws my back.

I yelp and twist around and throw a punch, and the mannequin's porcelain face explodes into pale dust. Into snow.

All the mannequins turn to snow, and snow drifts down around me in the courtyard. The courtyard with its bent trees and frozen fountain and bone-white mansion stretching up in the darkness beyond. Everything in the courtyard is white and frozen, snow drifting down peacefully, and in the heavy silence of the snow I hear my heartbeat slow. I feel the panic subside.

What was I running from?

*Where* was I running from?

I turn slowly on the spot, looking out at the gnarled trees and the mansion that looks so, *so* familiar, and when I make a full circle I see a figure standing before the fountain, facing away.

A figure in a wedding dress as white as the snow.

A figure that makes my skin go as cold as the snow.

She is crying.

Despite myself, my feet move forward, as if pulled on strings. I walk toward her, my feet crunching on ice, and even though my footfalls are loud, she doesn't turn to look at me. She doesn't seem to know I'm there.

I don't know why I do it.

"Are you okay?" I ask. She doesn't respond, and still my feet move me closer.

I reach out when I'm near. Touch her shoulder. It is hard and firm. Like ice.

Like porcelain.

And when she whips about to face me, her frozen fingers clutching my arms, I know my mistake.

The mannequin clutches me in her hands. Her

veil billows back, revealing nothing but shadows and smiling teeth.

I scream as her mouth widens and swallows me whole.

# 8

**I feel strange all through school.**

I'm on edge. Jumpy. Maybe it's because I woke up with a pounding headache and the feeling that I didn't actually get any sleep. Maybe it's because Patricia keeps smiling at me from her desk like she's up to something. Maybe it's because today, we're setting up for real, and for the first time this year, I'm worried that we won't be able to pull it off. Or maybe it's because I woke up tangled in my sheets and covered in sweat, running from a nightmare I can no longer remember.

For some reason, though, every time I see movement from the corner of my eye, a chill races down my spine. And I expect to see a woman in a white wedding dress.

Every once in a while, I think I do.

By the time school is out, I'm jumping at everything. The final bell rings, and I grab my stuff and head to my locker. Once my bag is packed, I slam the locker and race to the front door to find my friends.

I nearly stumble flat on my face when I pass by the science room door. Someone is staring through the window at me.

A woman in a white dress.

When I look back, however, there's no one there.

"Are you feeling okay?" Julie asks later, as we make our way to Corvidon Manor.

I nod. I don't like lying to Julie, but I don't want her worrying about me either. She's been my best friend since third grade, and even though she's not quite as into haunted houses as I am, she has always supported my passion. Even if it meant putting herself in creepy situations.

She *hates* being scared. Which means she's usually a good judge for whether or not we got the scares right.

"Just tired." I yawn, accentuating my statement. The trouble is, the yawn isn't faked—I don't think I slept at all last night. At least, not *well*. "I was up too late thinking about the haunted house."

This, I think, should sound believable. I don't want her to know I was researching the bride. I don't want her to get curious. I still haven't figured out how I'm going to surprise them with the mannequin's eventual appearance in our display. I still have to figure out how I'm going to acquire it without Mr. Evans noticing.

Julie smiles, but I can tell that *that* is faked. She doesn't say anything for a while. When she does, her words are hesitant and her voice quiet.

"Do you sometimes think that—" She cuts herself off.

"What?" I ask.

She looks at me. I can tell that—despite her bravado—she's worried.

"Well . . . every year you plan this big, huge, amazing room. And every year you work yourself sick to make it perfect."

This is true. I've just come to expect that the entire week after the haunted house's opening, I'll be out with a cold. Last year, I got a full-blown flu. My dads said it was because I worked too hard and didn't sleep enough.

"Yeah, but this year I'm prepared," I reply. I hold up the bottle of orange juice I've been chugging since we left the school. "Lots of vitamin C."

"And still no sleep," Julie replies. She raises an eyebrow. "I just don't want you hurting yourself over this. I know how Patricia gets under your skin. It's happening already."

"It's not about her." I take a swig of orange juice as if I'm making a point. The truth is, I'm pausing because I'm trying to think of what to say. Julie knows when I'm lying. Most of the time.

"It's about pride," I finally say.

I look around and take in the orange trees and crisp wind. It's a perfectly cool day, sweater weather, and it's days like this when I actually love being from New England. The chilly fall nights and fresh apple cider and pumpkins everywhere. It's one of the few times when living in a small town is fun.

The trouble is, that's only for a few months out of the year. Summers are muggy and filled with mosquitos and the winters are twenty feet of snow and the time in between is just mud. It's more than that, though. It's the fact that everywhere I look, I see someone I know: Mrs. Haverson sweeping leaves from her front drive, the Bruxley twins throwing a football across the road, Pete Mills smoking a pipe in front of his hardware store. I've seen everything in this town and this town knows everything about me.

Nothing exciting or new ever happens here. And that's another reason why I love the haunted house. Not only because it's my passion. Not only because it's what I want to do when I grow up. But because it's something new and exciting in this sleepy town, and being a part of it means that, I don't know, I'm responsible for it. I have to bring my A game to show this place something new. To keep things fresh so people don't die of boredom.

Myself included.

I try explaining this to Julie, but my words keep tumbling over my tongue. By the time I've finished, it's pretty clear that I haven't convinced her of anything. It's nothing I haven't said before, and she can hear the words that I don't want to say: *I have to do this to prove to Patricia that I am worth something.*

My dads both work full-time, and even though we do okay, we don't have as much money as her family, and she'll never let me forget that. I'm tired of her scoffing at our decorations, tired of her telling me that her new phone is nicer, or that she just went on a vacation to Hawaii when we didn't go on a vacation at all. I'm tired of her telling me that she is better than me because she has more money.

Once, she even laughed at my packed lunch, saying that she *didn't know how poor people could live like that*. I've never been so insulted.

At least, not until the competition last year.

It's like, every time I try to do something cool, Patricia either messes up what I've done or goes and just buys something cooler.

Case in point: The moment Julie and I arrive at the manor is the moment Patricia's mom drops her off in their shiny new convertible. No one needs a car like that in Vermont. I doubt it even has four-wheel drive.

"Do you like it?" Patricia calls out when her mom drives off. "It cost a fortune."

"It's a car," I say back. I nod to the boxes scattered around her. There are at least a dozen, and half of them are clearly new decorations. Cabinets with motion sensor–activated sound and movement, so they give the illusion of dolls trying to escape. Remote-controlled rats with glowing green eyes. Fog machines with built-in laser light shows, with scenes of lightning and ghosts preprogrammed. It makes my stomach clench. It makes me want to be mean. "Did your mom kick you out?"

Patricia just smiles sweetly. "Oh no. These are just some decorations. The first load. My dad is coming back with a moving van for the other five. I'm assuming you're just using the junk I saw down there earlier?"

*It's not junk.* "No, my dads are bringing the rest of our stuff soon, too."

She laughs.

"And I'm sure you'll have just *tons* of garbage. Is that what you're making this year? A haunted dump? No, wait, that's just your house."

I open my mouth, but Julie puts her hand on my arm to stop me from saying something I might regret later.

"Come on," she says. "We have a lot of work to do."

I let her drag me away and toward the manor. Something moves in an upstairs window. A flash of white. I don't really see it, but it still makes my skin crawl.

"Why even bother?" Patricia calls out, distracting me from the hallucination. "You're just going to lose again anyway."

I don't respond. I won't give her the satisfaction.

"You're grinding your teeth," Julie whispers as we reach the door.

"I hate her," I reply.

I take another drink of orange juice and try to relax. I'm *not* going to let Patricia get the better of me and throw me off my game. I'm *not*.

The trouble is, I know she already has.

# 9

Tanesha is already in the basement hanging lights when we arrive. The skeletons are all along one wall like soldiers, and just seeing them makes me shiver. It doesn't help that she starts testing the strobe light she's hung the moment we step down there.

In the flickering flashes, it looks like the skeletons are writhing. Their heads shaking, their jaws clacking, their arms reaching. But it's just the strobe. Right?

I watch one of them, entranced.

I watch as its eye sockets start glowing green, and I swear it begins clattering its teeth, mouthing my name . . .

"Kevin," it growls in its feminine voice. *"Kevinnnn—"*

"Kevin!" The voice changes. No, wait, that's Tanesha. She stands in front of me and waves her hand in front of my face. "Earth to Kevin, are you in there?"

I shake my head and look away from the perfectly normal, perfectly still skeletons.

"What? Sorry. Distracted."

"Clearly," she says. She peers into my eyes. "You're not getting sick already, are you?"

"No, I'm fine." I bat her away and try to smile.

"He just isn't sleeping," Julie pipes in.

"Let me guess," Tanesha says, looking to Julie. "He ran into Patricia."

Julie nods. I groan.

"Let's not talk about it," I say.

Except, of course, they want to talk about it.

"It's not the amount of money you spend that matters," Julie says. She places her hand on my chest. "It's about heart."

"And you, my friend, have one twisted heart." Tanesha smiles when she says it. It's probably the nicest thing she could say right now.

"Thanks," I say. I try to mean it. "You two are the best."

"And together, we're going to annihilate the competition," Tanesha says. She holds out her hand. "Because who are we?"

My smile widens and becomes sincere. I place my hand on top of hers. Julie puts hers on top of mine.

"The Bloody Banshees!" we yell out in unison.

We collapse into giggles.

Along the wall, so, too, does a skeleton.

# 10

Julie screams and Tanesha gasps and all I can do is stare in horror as a skeleton along the wall crumples to the ground in a pile of bones, laughing sinisterly.

For a while, we just stare at it, our mouths agape.

Then another picks up the laughter, deeper than the first. And another, high-pitched and skin curling.

Another.

And another.

One by one they start laughing, cackling, a demonic chorus of caustic giggles, their eyes glowing green and their skulls clattering.

It feels like the laughter goes on forever. It feels

like it's worming its way into my skull. Snaring my brain.

And then, all at once, they turn to face us.

Eyes locked with ours, in unison they let out a long, terrifying wail.

I slap my hands to my ears, but the moment the scream starts it stops, cutting off like a razor's edge.

My friends and I stand there for ages. The silence around us is so deep, all I can hear is our frantic breathing. We stare at the decorations, entranced, waiting for them to cackle again.

*THUD*

Something thunks down above us, making us all wince and yelp.

"Sorry!" we hear someone yell out. Just one of the other teams, dropping something on the floor. How did no one upstairs hear that scream?

I laugh forcedly. The others do as well. Thankfully, the skeletons don't. But we stop chuckling pretty quickly. None of us can look away from the skeletons.

"What was that?" Tanesha finally asks.

"I don't know," I say. "But one of them did it last night."

I step forward slowly, gingerly, and it's then that I realize I am actually, just-a-little-bit, somewhat afraid. I honestly expect the skeletons to leap at me, but I tell myself that it's stupid. They're just plastic toys. Like everything else in this room of scares, they are perfectly explainable.

Even if I can't explain them right now.

I kneel down in front of the first skeleton that collapsed. My hand shakes as I reach out and poke the skull. It rolls away harmlessly.

"It must be a glitch," Julie says nervously. "They all have voice recorders, right? The first one must have just recorded laughter from the store or something, and the others all picked it up."

"Yeah," Tanesha says. "Makes sense."

I nod, but I don't answer.

I also don't tell them that none of the skeletons have batteries. I made sure of it.

Just as I don't tell them that the bones scattered at my feet no longer look or feel like plastic.

They're real.

## II

**I pack up the real bones as quickly as I can, trying not** to be grossed out by the fact that they're actually human. Julie and Tanesha go back to unpacking our boxes—I know that if they stand around, they'll only freak themselves out more. I even let them put on some bouncy pop music to lighten the mood. I don't tell them that it makes me feel better, too. Because if they learn I'm scared, they will be even more so.

But my brain is racing as I gather the bones.

How in the world did a real skeleton end up in our basement?

How did its eyes glow and make sound?

Everything in a haunted house has a logical explanation.

Everything, except this.

When I finally stand to head up the stairs to get rid of the bones, I don't have any answers. Just more questions. And I can't let those questions distract me from my goal. I just know that if I keep the bones in the basement, Julie and Tanesha will find out.

I have to get rid of the evidence as fast as I can.

I pause at the foot of the steps.

Shivers trickle down the back of my neck like ice water. Even with the music playing, all sounds seem to fade. The lights flicker and die out. Until it's just me in the dark and the silence, and it feels like it's no longer the basement, but a great expanse of nothingness.

And there, in the shadows, is a smudge of white.

"Why did you do it?" the voice cries out, thick with tears. A young woman.

The smudge moves closer. Becomes a figure dressed in white.

The bride. Her hands to her face.

She slowly lowers her hands.

"I just wanted to rest. Why did you hurt me?" she asks.

And there, behind her hands, isn't a face, but darkness. Terrifying darkness, and I suddenly feel dragged back to my dream. Only I'm not dreaming. I'm awake. I'm awake and the ghost bride is here and—

"Did you forget something?" Julie asks.

I snap back to reality. To the brightly lit basement filled with boxes and pop music and my friends. There's no bride anywhere.

I must really not have gotten enough sleep last night. I'm passing out on my feet.

I shake my head, but I can't think of any words with which to answer. I just head up the stairs, clutching the box of bones tight to my chest and hoping for no more surprises.

# 12

"Aww, don't give up now," Patricia says snidely from the porch. "You only just started."

I grimace and pause, halfway to the trash bin outside. Go figure that Patricia would be watching for me.

"I'm not giving up," I say. Even though I shouldn't have to say it—I would never give her that satisfaction.

"Then why are you throwing all your decorations away?"

"I'm not—" I growl. "Just, mind your own business, okay?"

"Why? It's so much more fun minding yours."

She tromps down the steps and comes closer. I take a step back.

"What are you hiding in there?" she asks. *"Bodies?"*

The bones rattle. I take another step back.

"Go away," I grunt. "Don't you have a space to poorly decorate?"

She laughs haughtily, tossing her perfect blond hair like she's an actress in a bad rom-com.

"Oh, we're taking a break until my mom gets back with the rest of our stuff."

She takes another step toward me. I try to back up farther but my heel hits a large stone. I stop before I tumble over and suddenly have to explain to Patricia what I'm doing with a box of human bones.

"You'd be better off giving up now," she says quietly. "Save yourself the embarrassment. Again. You don't stand a chance."

She flips open a flap on the box and peers inside momentarily. Then she rolls her eyes and turns around.

"I'm in the big leagues now," she says as she

walks away. "Have fun playing with your stupid plastic toys."

I want to yell something out, but there's nothing to say. Nothing that won't make her think that she's winning. Nothing that won't make me sound pathetic.

I grumble to myself and try to breathe deep and force down the heat in my cheeks. I can't lose focus. I can't. Lose. Focus.

Before she can say anything else or come back to inspect what are definitely not stupid toy bones, I turn and stomp the rest of the way to the trash bin.

Hastily, I toss the contents of the box inside and hope that no one comes looking and thinks the bones are from a crime scene. I glance around, but no one else seems to be outside. Well, save for Mrs. Harris across the street, but there's no way she could see anything—she's nearly blind.

"I'm in the big leagues, too," I say.

I peer over the trash lid, one last time. Mainly because I'm curious, but also because I refuse to believe what I saw in the basement.

Except, when I look inside, it's just normal plastic skeleton bones and frayed wires staring back at me.

The heat in my chest immediately turns to ice, all the blood rushing to my feet.

"What in the world is going on?" I whisper to myself.

Thankfully, the skeleton doesn't answer.

But as I turn around and head to the house, a figure in white vanishes from one of the top-floor windows.

# 13

Even after the creepy skeleton incident, we get right to work.

Patricia's taunting has lit a fire inside of me, one that a few unexplainable skeletons can't get in the way of. My dads bring their pickup filled with all the boxes I sorted through and loaded up before bed last night, and my friends and I immediately get to unpacking and organizing.

Tanesha takes over the haunted graves, setting out the tombstones and the pathways amid piles of pillows covered in fake grass and red leaves so they look like rolling hills. The skeletal hands reaching up through the debris is a nice touch. Julie wraps all the pillars in cardboard and tape and paper, turning them into gnarled tree trunks, complete with grasping branches and animatronic ravens. And I take the swamp, one of the more intensive sections of the graveyard. It's just a kiddie pool we got on clearance at the end of the summer, but I've spray-painted it black and lined the outer edge with foam and dirt so it looks like a swamp. Throw in a few air pumps from old fish tanks, some water, and a bit of dry ice, and *voilà*: a bubbling, steaming pool of muck. At least, I hope that's what it will look like. Right now it just looks like a badly painted plastic pool.

We have music playing in the background, but unlike all the other times when we hang out, we aren't singing along or talking. We are in work mode. There are only a few hours to get everything set out, and that means there's no room for messing around.

I grab a hose and start filling the swamp from a spigot in the wall, then move on to my new addition: a gazebo.

Really, it's just a few pieces of wood I'm going to paint white, but it will look like a little hut when I'm through, a shadowy archway with just enough space to hide the ghost bride. An archway the guests *have* to walk past to exit. I've had the image ever since waking up this morning. It will be the last scare the guests encounter, and I want it to be good. They'll walk past and the ghost bride will leap from the shadows with a vicious wail. I've already started writing up a script to tell the guests as I guide them through the cemetery. The story of the ghost bride will be front and center.

I just have to figure out how to get her from Mr. Evans's care. And how to convince my friends that it's a good idea to do it. I kind of doubt that *Patricia sabotaged us last year, so it's okay that we stole a prop this year* will do it.

"I did some reading last night," Julie says.

"Oh?" Tanesha chimes in. "You finally learned how?"

"Hah hah," Julie replies. "I was reading about the bride. You know, the one whose dress Kevin tore up yesterday."

*That* makes me really pay attention to their conversation.

"I didn't do anything to the dress!" I call out. I can feel my pulse in my chest; the moment Julie mentioned the ghost bride, I felt like I was going to be sick.

"Right. You just smashed her head apart. Much better." I look over to catch Julie rolling her eyes. "Anyway, I was reading up about her. It's a really sad story. Did you know that the family didn't just keep the wedding dress; they kept a mannequin dressed in the gown just because they couldn't bear letting their daughter go? Some people even say she was *buried* in the dress before her parents took it back. It's so sad."

"That's not sad—that's weird," Tanesha says. "And creepy. But creepy in a what-were-they-thinking sort of way."

"I don't know," Julie says, softer. "I thought it was sort of sweet. They wanted her memory to live on. You should have seen the pictures."

*She read the same article as me. Of course she did!* I swallow. They've brought it up. Time to see if they're on board with this change of plans.

"I think it's a good story," I say. "I mean, it's really creepy. And it happened right here in Happy Hills.

Honestly, I think it would be cool if we had her in the exhibit. That would really creep everyone out, especially if they knew the story."

"No way," Julie says. "That's just wrong. We should leave her be."

"What do you mean, *her*?" I ask. "It's just a dress on a mannequin."

"But she was *buried* in that dress," Julie says. "Doesn't that creep you out?"

"Yeah," I say. I look at Tanesha when I say it. I can't read her expression at all. "But that's the point, isn't it? I mean, if it scares *me* . . ."

"No way," Julie says. "I'm not going to be in the same room as that thing."

I sigh. A part of me wants to back down. She's right—it's creepy, and it's probably disrespectful. But the rest of me refuses to give in. *That* part tells me it isn't disrespectful at all. I'm putting her back on display. Introducing her story to an entirely new group of people. Isn't that better than having the mannequin locked away in a dusty storeroom?

Patricia's face floats in front of my vision, and that squashes any thoughts I might have had about backing down. I *know* the ghost bride story will win us this competition. I don't want to lie, but it's clearly the only way to win.

It worked for Patricia.

"Fine," I say. I lower my head. "But I want to do a ghostly bride anyway. I think it's a good story. I'll just go get a dress from the costume shop. I think I might have a spare mannequin in storage."

"Fine," Julie says. "Just so long as you promise it won't be the same mannequin. That thing creeped me out."

"Promise," I lie.

Tanesha catches my eye. I know *that* look all too well: She knows I'm not telling the truth.

Thankfully, she doesn't call me out on it.

We get back to work. Every once in a while, I catch Tanesha looking at me.

As if she knows that there's something creepy going on.

As if she knows that the ghost bride is a part of it, and I'm intent on bringing the story back to life.

# 14

"How is everything coming together?" Poppa Jared asks.

We sit around the dinner table eating spaghetti with homemade sauce and breadsticks and a big Caesar salad.

"Yeah," Poppa Blake continues. "Are you feeling good about everything?"

I grumble a "Yeah, fine," and continue eating my spaghetti. I hope that's enough for them to move on to the next subject, like how Poppa Jared's workday was or even if I have any homework tonight. Anything to distract them from asking about the haunted basement.

But of course they don't want to talk about something else. Not when it's all I've been wanting to talk about all year.

"What's wrong, Kevin?" Poppa Jared asks.

"Nothing, PJ," I say. It's our nickname for him. Poppa Blake is PB. PB&J. Made for each other, just like peanut butter and jelly.

They know me too well to let me get away with my lie. They can tell something's wrong.

"Let me guess," PB says. "I bet it's a person and I bet their name rhymes with Morticia."

"Oooh, good *Addams Family* reference," PJ adds.

I grumble and don't say anything, just slurp down more spaghetti. They're not wrong, but they're not fully right either. We didn't get nearly as much done as I wanted to today. I still haven't figured out how to sneak the mannequin out of the broom closet. I'm lying to my friends.

But, in the end, it *is* all Patricia's fault, so it's not like I'm lying to my parents, too.

"I'll take that as a yes," Poppa Jared says. He

looks over at Poppa Blake with a knowing eyebrow raise. He's got big, bushy eyebrows, almost as bushy as his beard, so that one eyebrow raise speaks volumes. They're worried. Again.

"Do you want to talk about it, bud?" Poppa Jared asks.

"No," I say. Then I sigh and put down my fork. I know they won't let this go, so I push the truth a little more. "It's just that it feels like no matter what I do, it won't be as good as what she does. Like, I could put on the very best display and it still wouldn't be as cool as hers because mine doesn't have all of her special effects. She has *everything*. What hope do I have?"

"A good haunted house is about more than special effects," Poppa Blake says. "It's about telling a story that gets under people's skin. And you're a master storyteller."

"Money can't buy talent," Poppa Jared says. He reaches over and pats my shoulder. "And you're the most talented kid I know."

"You say that because I'm your son."

PJ snorts. "These aren't mutually exclusive facts," he says. His smile switches to something more serious. "I understand your frustration, bud. Really, I do. But I promise you, anything you do will be loads better than something pulled from a box. Everything you create is amazing and terrifying, and this year we know to be on the lookout so Patricia doesn't sabotage you again. I've already talked to her parents."

I groan. *"Daaaad."*

"What? I wanted to get to know the competition. They know that if anything funny happens this time, we're bringing it up to the judges, and Patricia will be automatically disqualified."

That immediately stops my frustration.

"Really?"

"Really," Poppa Jared says. "No matter what, this year is going to come down to skill and skill alone. So don't worry yourself over Patricia. She relies too much on what her parents can buy her. But you . . . you rely on talent, and that will win every time."

I smile at my dads. I wasn't expecting to feel better tonight, not after Patricia's snide comments. But knowing that my family has my back makes me feel like I can take on the world.

We go back to eating our pasta, my dads finally

turning their attention to asking each other about their days. I tune them out, my thoughts naturally falling back to the haunted house. We have one more night to get everything perfect. One more night to figure out how to steal and install the ghost bride without anyone catching on. The last thing I need is for Julie to freak out—she'd never let me hear the end of it. I can practically hear her now . . .

Wait.

I don't actually hear anything. Not my dads talking or even eating.

I glance up.

At first, I don't really understand what I'm seeing. My dads are both still there, poised with their forks raised halfway to their mouths. Neither of them is moving, though.

And that's when I realize

they are both mannequins.

I gasp and jolt back in my chair, and then my eyes snap open and I'm crouched over my plate of pasta and *wait*—was I sleeping for that? Like, did I fall asleep while eating?

My dads look at me.

"You feeling okay, bud?" PJ asks.

I nod, but it feels like the biggest lie yet. What *was* that? I swear they became mannequins.

I'm reminded way too much of the photographs I saw from the paper last night, of the mannequin bride poised at the dinner table. Maybe that's why I dreamed it. Because that's what that was, right? I fell asleep without realizing it and had a brief, terrifying dream.

"You look like you could use some sleep," PB says.

"Yeah," I say. "I think you're right."

I also think that—if last night was any indicator— sleep won't happen for a long while.

# 15

**I dream I'm back in the manor.**

I'm heading down into the basement, the heavy door slammed shut behind me. My feet thud loudly on the wooden steps, echoing like rolling thunder. I don't want to go down there. But my feet lead me, even if my heart clambers to get out of my chest, clawing its way up my throat in fear.

The stairs roll down forever, shadows whispering past me like phantoms with every step. The hairs on my arms prickle upright. Everything in me screams to run away, *run away*. Everything except for my traitorous feet.

They keep
     walking.
          Closer.

               *Closer.*

And then, I'm there.

Suddenly, there are no steps. Just a yawning expanse of concrete that I know must be the basement floor. I keep walking. My bare feet scrape against the cement. Until it isn't cement anymore, but grass. Grass stretching out to all sides, grass rolling up and down in mounds. Grass pockmarked with stones.

Tombstones.

I trip over a small rock. Look down.

Not just tombstones: bones.

I want to scream, but I can't open my mouth. Just as I can't stop myself from walking forward, through the rolling cemetery. Fog slinks around my feet, cold and damp like the tongues of spectral dogs. I shudder. At least I can do that, even if I can't run away. My body at least knows that this isn't right.

I expect to hear the moans of ghosts.

The rattles of skeletons.

The crunch of dirt as zombies rise from their graves.

But the graveyard is silent. Deathly, ghostly silent. Except for my breath and the crush of my feet on the grass. That almost makes it worse. Every single fiber of my body is strung taut with anticipation that something is about to go terribly, horribly wrong.

Through the mist, rising up like a skeleton, is a bone-white tree. Beneath it, a small gazebo. Just seeing it multiplies my fear.

I can't go there.

I can't . . .

I do.

Up the creaky steps of the wooden pavilion, where fog curls so thick I can't see a thing. I stand there, by the steps, and finally my feet stop. Nail me into place.

The fog clears, and when it does, I realize I'm not alone.

A woman stands on the porch before me, facing away. Crying.

Her sobs echo over the graveyard. How did I not hear her before?

"Why?" she moans. *"Why!?"*

She turns to me, her hands still pressed to her face.

"Why did you do this to me?" she demands.

She lowers her hands, and in the place of her head is only darkness and broken ceramic pieces.

*"Why did you bring me back?"*

She howls, her scream piercing my chest. My legs unlock. I try to run.

But before I can take my first step, she latches on to my arm and drags me down to darkness.

# 16

The next day, I'm able to entirely ignore Patricia. She tries talking to me in the halls and, when that doesn't work, loudly drops hints to our classmates about what amazing things she has planned. But I don't even think about it. Partly because of the pep talk from my dads, and partly because there's no doubt in my mind that the mannequin bride is our key to victory. If it's enough to give me not one, but *two* nightmares—including some really creepy waking dreams—then it is more than enough to tell a terrifying tale to win over the judges. No matter what zany special effects Patricia has on her own floor.

And that means I have to figure out how to steal the mannequin from the broom closet without Mr. Evans noticing. My brain spins all day with plans, and by the time the final bell rings, I think I have it worked out. I just have to figure out a way to get Tanesha and Julie to help out without them realizing. They have to think this is a different mannequin.

Tanesha's mom drives us all to the manor so we can get a faster start. We arrive before anyone else does, and Mr. Evans opens the door for the three of us with his usual caring smile.

My stomach turns over with the thought of my plan, but if it all works out, he'll never even know the mannequin was missing in the first place. When he sees it in the display, I'll convince him it's not the original.

My plan should work.

No, it *will* work.

"Welcome, children," Mr. Evans says. "Are you all ready for tomorrow?"

"Almost," Julie replies.

"Just a few more tweaks and we're done," Tanesha says.

"Yeah," I pipe in, grateful for the way the conversation is going. "Maybe you could come down later and check it out. Be our trial run?"

Mr. Evans smiles.

"Oh, I don't know. You kids come up with some pretty spooky things, and my old heart can't take any more scares."

I pat him on the arm as he walks us to the basement door. "I promise you'll have fun," I say.

"Well, I suppose . . ." His smile widens. "I do always look forward to seeing what you kids get up to!"

"This year is going to be scarier than ever," I say proudly. "Just wait and see."

# 17

**As my dads said, the most important part of a haunted house** is telling a terrifying story, and mine is going to do just that.

You start at the pathway at the foot of the steps, the trail outlined with dim purple LEDs. First, you pass by the tombstones with their reaching hands and the animatronic skeletons (hopefully they don't malfunction like the first night), ducking under papier-mâché trees and hanging cobwebs while pre-recorded sounds of snickering bats and crackling limbs play in the rafters. We even have a fan set up for a chilling breeze. The path leads you deeper into the basement, around twists and turns that are hidden behind black trash bags, which are further disguised with more cobwebs and tree branches, so you never really know where you're about to go. Especially with Tanesha's expert lighting design and flickering, lightning-like strobes.

During the premiere, Julie and Tanesha will be dressed up as zombies and will patrol the paths, scaring unsuspecting visitors the farther in they get. Past the skeletons and the zombies, you reach the bubbling swamp. I managed to hide my old smoke machine in a fake rock so the swamp will be covered in a heavy fog, and small remote-control boats covered in lights will dart through the murk, looking like will-o'-the-wisps or ghastly ghouls. All the while I—the gravedigger—will be spinning the horrifying tale of the ghostly bride, who is stuck forever in the afterlife wandering this graveyard, looking for her missing fiancé.

At the very end, just when you think you're reaching the stairs and safe, you hit the gazebo.

It's just big enough for someone to stand under, with cobwebs hanging from the front and a thick black tapestry on the back as a door. More cobwebs and creepy lights cover it. Inside the archway, it's entirely dark.

The only way out is past.

And there, hidden in the shadows and attached to a motion-sensor arm, will be the mannequin in her wedding gown. You won't see her until she leaps out with a flash of strobe light and a recorded cackle. If she doesn't terrify the judges, nothing will.

At least, that's the idea. Right now we're still missing a few lights, and some of the tombstones aren't propped up properly, and there are more cobwebs to hang, and we need to mix food coloring and cornstarch in the swamp water so it looks murky.

And I need to get the mannequin from upstairs.

Nothing that a few more hours of work won't fix.

I try to remain optimistic. There's still a ton of work to do, and the haunted house isn't nearly as creepy with all the lights on. But it will be. Soon. It has to be.

The gazebo waits beside me, empty, waiting for the final puzzle piece.

I blink.

Light flickers.

The archway isn't empty.

The bride hovers there, her white dress billowing around her, her head in her delicate porcelain hands. Weeping. All I can hear is her weeping. Weeping as the air around me goes cold as ice, and I feel like I'm freezing. Drowning.

"Why couldn't you let me rest?" she asks. "Why? **WHY?**"

She lifts her head, revealing nothing but black space behind her veil.

Then frigid lake water spills from her broken neck, pouring to the ground and splashing toward me. I stumble, try to avoid the water that I know will freeze me to the bone. Just like it froze her, before her parents dragged her back to shore. She isn't crying anymore, but screaming. Screaming my name.

I take another step back.

But I'm too slow.

Water sloshes around my ankles. Cold as ice.

Cold as death.

Cold as—

"Are you swimming in the swamp?" Tanesha asks.

I jolt and look around. Sure enough, I'm standing in my kiddie-pool swamp, water sloshed up to my ankles. My heart is in my throat and I can still hear the ghost bride's scream ringing in my ears. But when I look around, she's nowhere to be seen. Just my friends, standing with their mouths open, as if they're worried I've lost my mind.

I'm starting to worry the same thing.

"Just, er . . . thought I dropped something."

"So you stepped in the swamp to get it?" Tanesha asks. Her eyebrow rises. Once more, she doesn't believe me. I'm honestly surprised she hasn't interrogated me. Yet.

I shake my head.

"Tripped."

"Right," Tanesha says. She and Julie share a look.

They don't ask me any more questions, though. They just go back to final decorations, mumbling that I better not get anything wet.

I step out of the swamp and start untying my shoes.

What in the world is going on?

The real show hasn't even started, and the haunted house already seems to be haunting *me*.

# 18

With thirty minutes to spare, we are ready for the test run. Everything's in place . . . except for the bride. But I'm going to have to wait for that.

The lights are focused and the smoke machine (finally) works and all the animatronic skeletons have performed without a single glitch. Everything seems to be running perfectly. More importantly, I haven't had another hallucination. It must be that. Must just be me not getting enough sleep or being overstressed or something.

I mean, there's no other rational explanation, is there?

"Is it time?" Tanesha asks. She practically bounces when she says it. I think she's as excited about this as me. She even painted her nails as ghosts to get in the spirit. Pun intended.

"I think so," I reply. "Do you two want to practice your scares?"

"Sure!" Tanesha says. Julie's agreement is a little bit more reserved.

We only have to perform opening night—the rest of the time, the house is open as a walk-through attraction on Friday and Saturday nights. Not many people come for the rest of the month. The majority of the town will be there for tomorrow night.

This is our chance to make sure everything works as it should, because tomorrow, the house opens for real.

I jog up the steps to find Mr. Evans.

I find Patricia instead.

"Running away?" she asks. She peers behind my shoulder. "Or are you opening the door so your team-mates can throw away more junk?"

I grit my teeth and remind myself of what my dads said: *Talent is more important than fancy props.*

"No, actually," I say, trying not to sound angry. "We're all finished. I was just going to find Mr. Evans; he asked to be the first to see it."

The last bit is a lie, but I don't care. I watch her face when I speak, hoping she'll be upset that someone wanted to see our exhibit first. Instead, she just shrugs.

"He's upstairs," she says smugly. "He's been helping us hang a few of our heavier props."

She looks around, though the kids who are transforming this floor are nowhere to be seen.

Patricia leans in to whisper: "He's already told us we have the scariest room he's ever seen."

Then she stands upright.

"I'll just go get him for you, shall I? Don't want to ruin our big surprise."

Then, with an infuriatingly innocent smile, she turns on her heel and bounds up the stairs, leaving me staring at my reflection in a mirror.

Something blurs at the corner of the frame and I turn away before I can see what it is.

I don't want to see the bride staring back.

# 19

Around me, I can hear the music and laughter of our opponents—the Masked Mummies—as they put the finishing touches on their ground-floor fun house. But I ignore them. Because right now, Mr. Evans is in the basement going for a tour of my haunted graveyard, and I have maybe five minutes to find the mannequin and slip it downstairs without him noticing. I told Julie to keep him by the swamp and show off the various lights and special effects.

She and Tanesha think I'm using the bathroom. I have to be fast. I have to hope Patricia is too busy upstairs to wander down and spy again.

As quick as I can, I make my way down the back corridor toward the broom closet. This part of the mansion is off-limits for decorating, and it's strange to see all the original furniture once more. I swear the hall tilts back here—it feels like walking on the deck of a ship. There are so many doors, but I vaguely remember which one holds all the excess stuff. We had to grab the vacuum from here last year to clean up some of the glitter Patricia had thrown over the floor of our lab.

Thankfully, the door isn't locked, and there's no mistaking the mannequin in the corner: She faces away from me, her long dress covered in dust and cobwebs. Seeing her there, facing away with a veil draped over her broken neck, brings my dreams back to focus. Suddenly, this is the very last place I want to be.

I try to take it as a good sign.

"Sorry," I mutter. Then, before I can talk myself out of it, I grab her around the waist and take her out of the storeroom. The mannequin is a lot lighter than I expect her to be. And much colder, too.

My heart thuds in my chest so loud I can

practically hear my pulse as I creep down the long hallway. I pause at every single noise or creak. I haven't thought of a good explanation for if Mr. Evans comes back early, or stops me on the stairs. Immediately, I kick myself for not thinking this through. Maybe I should have grabbed the mannequin while he was up looking at Patricia's stuff. But she went and got him before I could stop her, and how would I have known he was there in the first place?

Miraculously, I make it back to the basement steps without Mr. Evans or anyone else stopping me. I pause at the door and open it a crack, trying to make out the sounds below. I try to ignore it—it must be my overactive imagination or nerves—but I swear I feel the mannequin *breathe*.

Over the recorded sounds of crickets and thunder, I faintly hear Julie explaining how we made the water look so murky. Good. I need to get this thing hidden quick before I get discovered or drop and break it. If it keeps creeping me out, it might happen on purpose.

One step at a time, I make my way down into the

basement. My breath catches with every creaky step down, but there's no turning back now. I just have to get her to the back corner where I already have a few trash bags hanging as a changing area of sorts. I make it off the stairs. Around the corner of a hanging trash bag. I'm in the clear! The stretch from here to the changing area is completely hidden away by a trash bag wall and there's no way Mr. Evans would come back here.

Phew!

I take three steps in, and the bag behind me rustles. I stop cold.

"What are you doing?" Tanesha asks. Thankfully, she asks it quietly.

Slowly, I turn around and face my friend and teammate. She stands there in the makeshift hall with her hands on her hips and a very disapproving look on her face.

"I, uh—" I stammer.

She just shakes her head. "You're stealing the mannequin? I can't believe you."

"Just borrowing!" I whisper fiercely. "I'll put it back."

"Kevin . . ."

"I know, I know. But look at it! It's so creepy!"

I turn the mannequin to face her. She actually flinches away when I hold it out.

"Ugh," she responds. "You said you were going to get a replacement."

"I couldn't find one in time," I lie. It had to be this one. I've known it all along.

Tanesha looks like she's going to argue.

"Please," I say. "No one has to know. She's going to be hidden until the very end, and it's a quick jump scare. No one will really see it, and Julie and Mr. Evans are the only ones who'd recognize it. They'll believe us if we tell them it's a different one. Inspired by the basement bride."

"They'll believe you because you always tell the truth," Tanesha says. "At least, you *did*."

That stings.

"I know it's wrong," I say. "But I also know that this prop and the bride story are what will win. I have to beat Patricia this year. I *have* to."

Tanesha looks at me for a long time. Sizing me up. But she knows that I'm telling the truth about *this* at the very least. When we lost last year, I was torn up for weeks. Even *after* the illness, I couldn't eat or sleep or focus. It had felt like my dreams of getting out of here and doing something big with my life had been ripped from my hands.

She'd been the one comforting me and telling me that this year we'd win, no matter what. I can tell she's regretting it.

"Fine. Just . . . if anyone realizes this is the original mannequin, it's all on you. I want nothing to do with it. Got it?"

I nod.

"Thanks," I whisper. *For not telling on me. For still being my friend. I think.* I'm not so certain about the last part. I worry this might have taken it too far—lying not just to Mr. Evans, but to my friends. Then I remember Patricia's gloating earlier today, and the worry fades. Or at least turns from sickness to resolve. I have to do this. *Have* to.

Tanesha doesn't respond, just shakes her head and disappears back into the haunted basement. I think I hear her mutter, "Unbelievable," as she leaves.

Relief flooding through my veins, I lean the

mannequin carefully against the wall. I'll come in early tomorrow night to set her up, before the others get here.

"Tomorrow," I say to the mannequin as I drape a trash bag over her, hiding her almost completely.

When I turn to go, I hear a female voice whisper to my back.

*"Tomorrow."*

# 20

I'm so amped up on adrenaline for tomorrow that it takes forever to fall asleep. I don't even have the ability to feel afraid over what happened earlier—I've chalked up all the strange occurrences to electrical malfunctions or exhaustion-induced hallucinations. There's no such thing as ghosts or haunted mannequins or possessed dresses.

Everything is explainable.

Everything terrifying has a logical cause.

I can't let my imagination get in the way of us winning this competition.

And tonight, I have to ensure that I know precisely

what I will say tomorrow. I have to know the story of the ghost bride inside and out. So after finishing my homework, I spend my night rereading the articles from before. Trying to memorize the tragic tale of the drowned bride and her creepy parents.

Maybe it's that, or maybe it's my own creativity, but as the night grows heavier I start to feel the same eyes on the back of my neck as before.

I'm being watched.

I can even hear her breathing.

"Not going to work," I tell myself aloud. "I refuse to be scared by my own imagination."

The sensation fades. A little.

I read through the articles a few more times, and I start to understand what my friends were saying. I feel *sorry* for the ghost bride. She lost her fiancé, and then her family wouldn't even let her rest in peace. They kept her memory alive for eternity by creating the mannequin.

Maybe Tanesha was right. Maybe we should just let her be. There's still time to find another mannequin and another dress.

Then I think of Patricia's prank.

No.

It has to be the real thing. It has to be the true scare.

"What does it matter anyway?" I whisper. "She's dead. She doesn't care."

It's my imagination. I know it.

Somewhere, in the shadows of my room, I hear her whisper: *"But I do."*

I really, really need to get more sleep.

I flip off my computer and close my eyes, mentally walking through our cemetery installation and going over my lines.

As sleep creeps closer and my dreams take over, I don't even realize when I've stopped imagining and have fully started dreaming. Or maybe I am awake. It's hard to say. All I know is that as I imagine walking through our haunted graveyard, I'm no longer in a basement. The concrete beneath my bare feet begins to squish. Cold mud seeps between my toes and a biting wind cuts through the willows, their long branches scratching together like skeletal fingers.

I want to stop, but once more, my feet drive me forward. Over the hills and soggy glens, under the snapping branches of the willows. A full moon hangs heavy above me, just above the horizon, and thick clouds skirt against it in agitation. As if not even the clouds want to be out here.

In the far-off corner of memory, I worry that I am being led back to the gazebo. Back to the weeping bride and her cavernous maw. But my feet don't drag me down that dirt path. No, I am led as if on a string, through the soggiest bits of the swamp, marsh weeds brushing against my hips with every step.

Slithery things slink wetly around my ankles. I bite back a gasp as one hisses past me, fearing the sting of serpent teeth. Still, I keep going, through the infested mire. Murky water squelches up past my ankles. A new panic races through me.

What if I'm being led to the water to drown? What if I walk straight into the center and keep going, down into the deepest depths of the swamp, where the forgotten bodies of wanderers past float restlessly?

My path doesn't lead me into the bubbling swamp, however, but past it. I skirt the edge and soon the land rises again. Straight up I go, up a hill covered in nothing but grass. No trees. No tombstones. Not even wisps of fog dare tread here.

For some reason, the empty hill scares me more than even the snakes I walked through to get here.

Because inside the hill, vibrating up through my heels, I feel a heartbeat. Slow and ominous and deep.

*Thud*

*thud.*

*Thud*

*thud.*

*Thud*

*thud.*

I pant as I reach the top of the hill. My work isn't done yet.

I drop to my knees and dig my fingers into the soft soil, mud caking my nails.

*I don't want to dig.*

I don't want to unearth the heart, the beats louder with every handful of dirt.

*I don't have a choice.*

Soon, I am covered in dirt and grass and sweat, and even though the night is cold as winter my muscles burn and my chest is hot.

Faster
  and faster
      I dig,
  and faster
      and faster
          the heart races.

*Thud*
  **thud**
          *thud*
                **thud**
  *thud*
      **THUD—**

My fingers scratch against wood.
  A casket.
Rotten, moldy wood.
  I clear away more dirt, and between one handful
of dirt and the next, the coffin lid is clear.
  I don't know who lies inside.
                    *I know who lies inside.*
  I press my palm to the cold wood, and it gives like
cheese under my fingers. A hole, large enough to see
through.

When I see inside the casket, my lungs finally let out a scream.

And when the body within—my body, *me*—opens his eyes,

both the heartbeat in the hill
and the one in my chest

stop.

# 21

I wake up covered in sweat.

When I look at my hands, dirt cakes the under-sides of my nails.

# 22

All day at school, I have to fight off the faint trace of
fear that lingers in my veins.

I can't look directly into the bathroom mirrors—
I'm too afraid of what I'll see.

I can't look around corners, for fear of the flash of
a white wedding dress.

When Tanesha finds me after the final bell, I feel
like every nerve in my body is ready to snap. It doesn't
matter how many times I tell myself it's just my imagination, that it's a good sign—the dream sticks to my
thoughts, and even rational, logical me is having a
hard time pushing past the primal fear.

"You look like you're sick," Tanesha says. She presses the back of her palm to my forehead. "No fever, though. You feeling okay?"

"I didn't sleep," I explain.

I spent all of lunch in the library. Not because I wanted to do homework, but because being in crowds made me feel strange. I swore, every single time I walked down the hall or let my gaze relax in a classroom, I saw her, from the corner of my eye. A woman in white. Watching at the edges. Waiting.

"You're avoiding us," Tanesha says.

I shake my head.

"You are," she continues. She shoulders her bag and walks down the hall, heading toward the exit. I can see Julie farther on—she waves when she spots us. "It's about the mannequin. You're afraid to come clean to Julie."

"Shh," I reply. "I am not."

"Then I'll just tell her. Hey, Julie!" She holds up her arm in salute, and I slap it down.

"Don't! It's just . . . okay, yes. I don't want her to know it's the same mannequin. I know she wouldn't approve. You know how she feels about breaking the rules. And she already feels bad enough about using the bride's story."

"She's your teammate and she's going to find out eventually."

"Yes, but ideally not until much later."

Tanesha stops and looks at me.

"You're really willing to risk losing the trust of your best friend to win this thing?"

My mouth gapes.

"I . . ."

Julie bounces up to us, and whatever I was stumbling to say silences in my throat.

"Hey, guys!" she says. "Aren't you excited?"

She seems to catch the look that passes between Tanesha and me.

"What's going on? Are you feeling okay? Did I miss something?"

Tanesha shrugs.

"It's nothing. We were just talking about Kevin's plan to win this year. Apparently, he's learned a lot from Patricia."

She begins walking away. Julie stands there and looks between the two of us.

"What is she talking about?" Julie asks.

"Nothing," I say quickly. "It's nothing. Just opening-day nerves."

She nods, but it's clear she doesn't quite believe it.

I'm not becoming like Patricia . . .

Am I?

# 23

**While Julie and Tanesha get ready in the upstairs** bathroom, I guiltily put the finishing touches on our display.

I keep waiting for Patricia to come down and taunt me. In a way, I *want* her to come down. Because then I will know for sure that she is terrible and I am not.

But she doesn't, which makes what I'm doing feel so much worse.

Frantically yet gingerly, I attach the mannequin to the robotic arm with some zip ties and twine. I don't want to leave any marks on her. Thankfully, the mannequin is so light and the mechanism so sturdy—basically a few door hinges with a motor and sensor attached—that it takes only a few minutes to get her set up. I rearrange her dress and place a hollow wire frame I made out of coat hangers onto her neck. The wires are black and create a rough oblong shape; when I drape the veil atop it, it looks like it is being held up by a ghostly head.

For an even creepier effect, I hide a mini LED down the neck, so the entire interior glows a ghastly green. Thankfully, there aren't any more spiders hiding down there.

When I step back and admire my handiwork, a chill races down my skin.

She is terrifying.

The moment she is complete, she seems to take on a life of her own. She's not just a prop held up with wire and filled with lights. She has a *presence*. A sadness, almost; it chills the air and steals the breath from my lungs. It both scares me and makes me feel bad for her.

Perfect.

"We're going to win with you," I whisper to the bride. "Patricia doesn't stand a chance."

Tanesha's accusatory stare filters through my memory. I'm not becoming as bad as Patricia. I'm just borrowing a mannequin, not actively sabotaging anyone else's place. It's not my fault that Julie doesn't like breaking the rules. If she were a little bit braver, I wouldn't have had to hide this from her.

No matter what I tell myself, however, I can't feel good about it. I just have to try to convince myself that she will be okay with it. That she'll understand what winning means to me.

She's my friend.

Of course she'll understand.

Mildly heartened, I turn away and grab my bag of costume supplies. I'm just dressing as a caped gravedigger, so all I need is a cloak and shovel and some eyeshadow.

Behind me, I hear the *swoosh* of the mechanical arm moving the mannequin back into hiding. She's already working perfectly.

Tonight we'll win the trophy, and even if Julie's angry, she'll soon forgive me after having all the free pizza and ice cream she can handle. For a whole year.

It's just a borrowed prop.

What could possibly go wrong?

# 24

We gather in the long hallway leading to the front door. All four teams.

The Masked Mummies, who created the fun house on the ground floor, are all true to name—they're wrapped in bandages splattered with blood, but rather than traditional pharaoh masks, they're all wearing terrifying clown masks. Then there's the Creepy Crawlies, who made the toy factory on the second floor; they're all dressed as large, creepy toys—a teddy bear with claws and fangs, a unicorn with no eyes and a bloody horn, and a large, terrifying doll with blank black eyes.

Then there are my true rivals, Patricia's group, who are doing a haunted labyrinth in the attic: the Monster Mashers. Their costumes are a lot less original. Patricia is dressed all in black, with ghoulish white face paint and claw gloves on her hands. Her friends are even simpler—one is a ghost, just a white sheet, and the other is wearing a skeleton costume.

A small part of me wonders if these are just disguises, and they'll change into their real costumes upstairs. I mean, this can't be her winning idea, can it?

Julie and Tanesha stand by my side in their full zombie makeup. Tanesha has a fake eye hanging from her socket and Julie has one hand hidden behind her back under her tattered clothes, with a fake arm clutched in her free hand. Their makeup is perfect— sallow and bruised, complete with fake gashes and protruding bones.

"You look terrifying," I whisper to them.

Julie smiles at me. Tanesha's expression is more of a grimace. It makes me think I should have put a little more effort into my own costume. I just sort of look like a goth kid with a cape and a shovel. Maybe I'll give myself a hunchback.

Mr. Evans clears his throat, and we all go silent.

"All right, children," he says broadly. He's dressed up like Frankenstein's monster, complete with fake bolts coming out of his neck and a tall, flat skullcap. "You all know the rules. I'll give you ten minutes to get to your places and ready yourselves. Then the judges will come through and begin their rounds. They'll start down in the basement and work their way up to the attic, judging each attraction as they go."

"Saving the best for last," Patricia whispers in my ear.

I jolt. I didn't even realize she was standing behind me.

*That's what you think*, I tell myself. It doesn't make me feel any better. Tanesha stares over at me. I know what she's thinking: *You're no different. Maybe you two should work together next year.*

"After the judges go through, we will ring the gong"—he points to a big gong beside the door— "which will signal that the judging is over. From there, the house will open to the public for another two hours. We ask that you stay in your respective areas for the entire time." I can't help but notice that he looks directly at Patricia when he says it.

At least, I *think* he's looking at Patricia. Maybe he's looking at me. Maybe he knows . . .

"You've all done a great job this year. No matter what, you should all be proud of yourselves. So, let's have one big cheer for teamwork, and for Halloween bringing us all together."

We all give a big "Hip, hip, hooray." My heart thuds so fast in my chest I feel it might burst. But this time, it's not with fear. It's with sheer excitement.

This is the moment I've been waiting for all year.

This is it.

Mr. Evans waves us on, and we all scatter to our respective floors.

I hear the door open and close behind me as we head toward the basement, and Mr. Evans's booming voice as he announces to the waiting crowd that we are almost ready to begin.

Then the basement door closes behind us, and the rest of his speech is swallowed up by darkness.

# 25

**Minutes creep by.**

I check my watch: 6:06. The doors will have opened by now. The judges must be on their way.

I stand at the base of the stairs, hiding behind a papier-mâché tree, my shovel in hand and my hood pulled high. My heart beats so loudly I can't hear anything besides my pulse, not even the crickets or the storm noises we have playing on repeat. A crackle of thunder crashes through the speaker, along with a well-cued strobe flash.

Are those footsteps I hear above me?

The judges must be getting close.

I hunch over.

I'm ready.

So.

Ready.

Something creaks above me. They're here! Yes! It's time to go.

I raise my shovel, which is our signal that the judges are arriving. Farther in, I know that Tanesha and Julie begin their prowl, moaning low and menacingly.

The door doesn't open.

Another minute passes.

What's taking them so long?

I check my watch. 6:15.

My excitement turns sour. Did the judges get mixed up? Are they going to the attic first?

I can practically see Patricia smiling to herself up there as the judges tour her room first. I bet she got her parents to bribe the judges to go upstairs. She's hoping to throw us. Thinking we'll break character to go investigate and thus lose by default. Well, I'm perfectly fine waiting. I'm not going to let her get to me. When the judges come down, we'll be ready.

I check again: 6:20.

Okay, even if the judges did go from the top down, they should be reaching us by now. I see Tanesha amble by. She gives me a very clear *What the heck is going on?* look. I shrug.

At least she and Julie haven't broken character. They really are professionals. Much better actors than I am.

Footsteps echo above us. Running. *Huh.* Maybe that's part of the fun house's display, like chasing clowns or something. It makes me grateful I'm not a judge—I *hate* clowns.

The thudding footsteps reach the basement door, and suddenly the door is thrown open, slamming on its hinges, and more footsteps crash down into the basement. I peer up from my hiding place.

It's not a judge.

It's Patricia.

I take a step forward and feel anger rise in my chest.

"What are you—?" I begin.

Then I see the look on her face.

Fear.

Pure, absolute fear.

"Guys, come quick," she gasps. "The house . . . the rooms. They're haunted. *They're real!*"

# 26

For a moment, all I can do is stare at her.

Then I start to laugh.

"Really?" I ask through my laughter. "That's your big plan? *That's* how you intend to sabotage us?"

"Kevin, I'm not—"

"And I'm not buying it, Patricia! You aren't going to make us break character and lose this. I bet the judges are right behind you." As if on cue, I hear footsteps upstairs. "Now, go back to the attic before the judges come down and you ruin everything. You know that my dads talked to the judges, and if you're caught trying to sabotage us again, you're disqualified."

Patricia doesn't drop the act. Her wide eyes look up to the door.

"It's not the judges. Mr. Evans never came back in. No one did. We're trapped in here, Kevin, and the rooms have come alive! We have to try to escape!"

"What's going on?" Tanesha asks. She steps up beside me. "What are *you* doing down here?"

"Trying to get us disqualified," I say. "She says the rooms have come alive."

Tanesha laughs. "Wow. That's pathetic." She shakes her head and looks to me. "What time is it? I feel like the judges should be here by now."

"Guys, listen to me!" Patricia yells. She reaches out and grabs my shoulder. Hard. "This isn't a joke! The judges aren't coming! This. House. Is. *Alive!*"

I reach up to shove her hand off my shoulder. To tell her this nonsense is getting old.

That's when I hear Julie scream.

# 27

Tanesha and I stare at each other for a second, and then, without speaking, take off toward the sound of Julie's screams.

"Don't leave me!" Patricia calls out behind us. "Please!"

But we're off. Crashing over foam and papier-mâché, pushing aside draped garbage bags. Thunder rolls above us, a great booming roar. Strobe lights flash.

My foot catches on something hard and I stumble. Crash to my knees.

And sink into wet, musty earth.

My heart leaps into my throat as I stare down at the grass poking wetly between my fingers.

"What in the world . . ." I whisper. We didn't bring any real grass down here.

Tanesha gasps at my side. "Kevin. *Look*."

She points.

When I raise my head I'm hit with a soul-crushing truth.

Foggy swampland stretches out around us, filled with real willow trees and a heavy moon resting above their branches. I look back to what I tripped over.

A tombstone.

A real, broken tombstone.

We're in a graveyard.

# 28

Tanesha helps me to my feet, but we don't race off again. We stand there, surrounded by heavy mist, tombstones rising from the fog like demonic hounds.

"What is going on, Kevin?" Tanesha asks. Her voice is surprisingly calm. Like she's in shock.

"I don't know," I reply.

I look behind us. I don't see the basement steps anymore, but I know they were back there. At least, I think they were. I hope.

"This is a real graveyard," she says. Not a question. Her statement is tinged with disbelief.

"Yeah," I say. My brain feels like it's stalled. Where

thought should be is just one long high-pitched ring.

"We have to find Julie," Tanesha says. She takes a step forward.

I'm frozen.

Anything could be out there.

But that's not why I don't want to move. Suddenly, my dreams from the past few nights flood back through my thoughts.

The hill with a casket holding my own body.

The swamp filled with snakes.

The pavilion with the weeping bride.

I know precisely what's out there, and for the first time in my life, I'm really, truly scared.

I try to move my feet, but they are stuck to the ground. How is this happening? How are we here? How can this be real? Absolutely nothing about this is explainable or rational or logical, and it feels like my brain is short-circuiting, because, somehow, *this is no dream.*

Julie screams again, closer this time, and my legs finally kick into gear. Tanesha hurries on beside me. Together, we race through the fog in search of her.

Tombstones tumble under our feet, but we

manage to leap over them. This part of the cemetery is just rolling hills and graves, though the grass squelches under our feet with the promise of swampland. Somewhere out there is the mire, and the snakes, but for now at least we race over dry land. I hope I never have to encounter one of those snakes in real life.

Or the bride.

Or the hill with my casket . . .

"There!" Tanesha yells out. She points ahead, to the top of a hill.

A lone, scraggly tree scratches up to the moonlight. And at its base, cowering against the trunk, is Julie. She holds a branch in both hands, swinging it at the fog.

I push for extra speed, but Tanesha reaches out and grabs my arm, forcing me to slow down.

"Kevin," she gasps. "What are *those*?"

Because there, stumbling through the mist, are shambling gray shapes my brain doesn't want me to see. I know them from their hunched backs,

their outraised arms,

their lumbering gait.

I know before their moans even hit my ears.

"*Zombies*," I whisper.

"No way," Tanesha replies. But now she sounds like she's finally panicked. "What do we do?"

I look at her. She's staring at me in a way that tells me she expects me to take the lead.

"I don't know," I reply.

*I build haunted houses, not live in them!*

"But you've watched all sorts of scary movies," she replies. "You have to know how to defeat them."

My mind races. I *have* watched a lot of scary movies. That's how I get a lot of my material. But there's a difference between *watching* a scary movie and *being* in one.

Especially because, in scary movies, the main characters often do everything wrong.

"Zombies are slow and kind of stupid," I say. "Maybe one of us can distract them while the other runs in and saves Julie."

"I'm fastest," Tanesha says. It's not a fact she seems happy about right now. She swallows hard. "I'll distract them. You save Julie."

I nod. Look around. "Let's meet back by that

tree," I say, pointing in the direction from which we came.

She nods once and darts off, cutting through the mist like an arrow.

"Hey, zombies!" she calls out. "Over here! Look at me! I bet my brains taste delicious!"

The zombies groggily look over to Tanesha, who stands a few yards away from them, jumping up and down and waving her hands. They're the real deal—they even *smell* dead. Some are missing arms, others don't have jaws or eyes. There's even one that's just a torso on the ground, scratching toward Julie with bloody hands.

For a moment, I don't think our plan is going to work. Then Tanesha yells out again, and they start hobbling toward her.

She immediately runs away. The zombies follow.

I run up to Julie as quietly as I can. She's slouched against the tree, and when she sees me, she raises the branch as if to hit me with it. Thankfully, she sees it's me right before striking. She drops the branch and jumps toward me.

"Kevin!" she yelps. "I was so scared. I was just

walking around acting like a zombie and then—"

"Shhhhh," I urge. I pat her on the back and look around wildly, but it seems like the zombies are still preoccupied with Tanesha. I see her running circles around them farther off. "Stay quiet. We don't want to be found."

She gulps and nods.

"Can you run?" I ask.

Another nod.

"Good. Because we're getting out of here."

*I hope.*

# 29

Julie and I wait at the meeting point for what feels like hours. She holds the branch and I clutch a piece of tombstone and we stare out through the dark mist in quiet fear. Every once in a while, lightning crackles overhead, and the graveyard is illuminated in the flash.

It stretches on forever.

I don't tell Julie, but I worry I won't be able to find our way back. If there even *is* a way back.

Fog creeps closer and higher, until the next time lightning flashes, I can't see anything but gray. Chills race down my skin, and not just from the cold, damp mist.

"Kevin," Julie whispers. "Do you think she's okay?"

"Yeah," I reply. I try to sound brave and assured, but I'm secretly worried. Tanesha should have been back by now. What if she got lost in the fog? What if she never finds us? What if she was—? "She's fast and she's smart," I tell Julie. "Those zombies don't have a chance."

Julie doesn't say anything. Every other sound gets swallowed up by the mist.

Lightning flashes again. Something dark is backlit in the fog. Coming toward us.

I press even closer to the tree and hold an arm out protectively over Julie. My eyes are wide. I can't see anything after the lightning. I can't tell if it's a zombie or a monster or—

"Tanesha!" Julie cries. She flings herself forward and hugs our friend. Tanesha looks winded, but unscathed. Her makeup is smudged and the fake eyeball has fallen off somewhere mid-run.

"You made it," I say.

"Course I did," Tanesha replies. "Got lost in the fog trying to find you guys. You sure this is the right tree?"

I open my mouth and then see that she's kidding. I let out a forced laugh.

"We need to get out of here," Julie says. "What if they come back?"

Suddenly, even my strained humor fades.

"I think we go this way," I say. I point toward the direction that I *hope* is the stairs.

"You think, or you know?" Tanesha asks.

I want to say *I know*, but I don't want to lie again. Clearly, my hesitation is answer enough.

"Better than nothing I guess," she says, and begins trekking through the cemetery.

I keep my eyes peeled for zombies as we go. Lightning flashes, but so far, I don't see any monsters. Just an endless, churning mist dotted with spindly black shapes that I hope against hope are only trees and not giant skeletons. Hopefully, Tanesha led the zombies far, far away from here. Hopefully, we'll find the stairs and be able to leave and this—whatever *this* is—will be all over.

"What if we can't find the stairs?" Julie whispers.

Her words thrill me with fear; that's exactly what I'm worried about.

"We will," I say reassuringly. "I'm sure of it."

That, at least, I'm okay lying about.

# 30

I don't know how long we wander through the fog. Past tombstones with scratched-out names. Under trees with branches like claws. The moon doesn't move in the sky, and when I check my watch, it's saying it's midnight. Which can't be possible. Can it?

"Eventually, someone's going to look for us," Julie says as we wander.

I know she's just trying to convince herself, but it does make me feel a little better.

She's right. Eventually, the adults will realize something is wrong, and they'll hammer down the door or break through the windows and there will be search teams and tracking dogs and everything. We'll be safe.

"*If* they can get in," Tanesha says. She looks at me. "You heard what Patricia was saying. The house is locked. We can't get out. And that means no one can get in."

"Don't think like that," I say. "Negative thinking doesn't help anyone."

"Not negative," she replies. "Just honest. Besides, I think it's better if we don't rely on adults to help us. Waiting for help to come doesn't do anyone any good when something's after you. We have to do this on our own."

"We still don't know what any of this *is*," I say.

"No. But once we find the other kids, we'll figure it out." She peers through the fog, and her skeptical look breaks into a smile. "There, look! I see it!"

I squint. And there, through the fog, I see what looks like a small, oddly shaped pyramid. My heart leaps into my chest. The stairs! And there's a figure at the base that must be Patricia.

"Come on!" I yell.

Julie yells at my side, but it's not from excitement. She's looking behind us.

To where the zombies are shambling forward, a lot faster than they were before.

"Are they . . . running!?" Tanesha yelps.

My heart flips in fear; she's right. The zombies are running toward us, arms outstretched and their gray skin flashing in the moonlight. I can hear their moans now, and the trample of their feet on the earth. Dozens of them. Hundreds. Stretching out through the mist as far as I can see. And they're gaining on us. Fast.

"RUN!" I yell.

We bolt. Straight toward the steps, holding each other's hands. I can only hope that none of us stumbles, sprains an ankle, or worse.

I don't want any of us to be eaten by a zombie.

My breath burns in my throat, and it feels like the stairs are getting farther

and farther

away.

My toe catches on a stone.

I stumble

but Tanesha's firm grip keeps me steady.
We run.

       Panting.

   Terrified.

The zombies

      are

         so

            close

I can hear their grinding teeth

   and crunching bones.

      I can smell their decaying flesh.

We're not going to make it.

        *We're not going to make it!*

"Hurry!" Patricia yells.

She stands near the base of the steps, and it's then that I realize there's a doorway at the very top. A doorway leading to nowhere.

We put on speed and reach the stairway.

We stumble up the wooden steps.

Patricia urges us on and in. I barely have time to wonder how I see a hallway in the doorway before jumping through. The last thing I hear is the slam of a door behind me and the pounding of fists on the frame.

# 31

The four of us huddle against the far wall, panting and frozen with fear as we stare at the door and hope that it holds. Zombie fists continue pounding. Their hungry moans pierce through the wood, and their shadows stretch under the door frame.

But the door holds.

The knocking fades.

And finally, after what feels like an hour, the hall falls into silence.

"What was that?" Julie asks. Her timid voice sounds far too loud.

I glance left and right. Nothing in *here* seems to

have changed. The hall stretches from one end of the manor to the other, lined with armoires and bookshelves and closed doors. We're near the back, but there, near the front door, is a huddle of shadowed shapes.

"What's in the basement?" someone calls from the door.

"Zombies!" Patricia calls back.

Whoever asked mumbles something; they don't sound happy.

"Who's that?" I whisper to Patricia.

"Ed," she replies. "From the Mummies. We're trying to rally everyone together, but . . ."

"But what?" Tanesha presses.

"But we can't find everyone," Patricia says. She looks to me, and I'm surprised to see there are actually tears in her eyes. "Lily from my team is missing. The Creepy Crawlies are still lost. And Ed and James are the only ones from the Masked Mummies who made it back."

She swallows, hard.

"What exactly is happening here?" I ask.

"I don't know," she replies. She sinks back against

the wall, and it's the first time I've seen her not look angelic or demonic. She looks like a kid, just like the rest of us. Scared and confused and in a bad costume.

In that moment, she doesn't seem like an enemy, and I don't quite know what to do with that.

"We were all getting ready for the judges to show up. It was Ed who first realized something was wrong—he was waiting by the front door in hiding. The judges never showed, so after a few minutes he tried opening the door to see what was up. It didn't budge. And when he went back to talk to his teammates, he realized it was . . . well . . ."

Patricia gulps.

"He opened the door to his room and it was filled with creepy clowns and carnival music. He slammed it shut immediately and ran up to try to find us. Thankfully, James had been waiting for him at the door for updates."

For a moment, I feel a pang of anger that Ed didn't come to the basement first. But then again, if I had just seen a room of creepy clowns, the basement is probably the last place I would have wanted to run.

"We tried gathering everyone we could," Patricia says. "That's why I went to get you. But we can't get far into the rooms without getting lost. I don't know what's going on, but it's like all of our themes came alive. The attic has become a real labyrinth. The second floor is like some possessed toy factory. And then you have your graveyard . . ."

She trails off. None of this makes sense.

"How could this be happening?" Julie asks. "How could this be *real*?"

"I don't know," Patricia says. "But we have to find a way out of here. Before we all get trapped forever. Or worse."

# 32

Eventually, we gather ourselves and head to the front door. Ed and the others are stationed there, huddled in their costumes like sad trick-or-treaters.

"It's locked," Ed says when we near. He's still in his bandages, but he's taken off the creepy clown mask. He wiggles the handle to prove his point: The door doesn't budge.

"What are we going to do?" Julie asks.

"We have to find a way out of here," Ed says. "I've tried the back door but it's locked, too. And we can't break the windows. We tried. They're like steel."

The front door is mostly an ornate stained-glass

window; it looks like it would shatter if we breathed on it too hard. But I don't doubt Ed one bit. I press up to the window and look out through one of the blocks of stained glass. Outside, everything is obscured in fog.

"I can't see anything," I say.

"Yeah," Ed replies. "All the windows are like that. It's like we're . . . I dunno. It's like we've been transported somewhere else."

One of the kids—James—is rocking back and forth with his knees curled to his chest, mumbling over and over, "This can't be happening." It isn't making me feel any better.

"So even if we *do* get the door open," I say, "there's no telling what we're going to find out there."

"What are you saying?" Patricia asks.

"I'm saying that our first priority needs to be finding the others. We can split up. Take our own floors since team leaders should know the layout."

I regret the words the moment they leave my mouth. The last thing I want to do is venture deeper into this nightmare. Now it seems like we don't have a choice.

"What about the second floor?" Ed interjects. "No one from the Creepy Crawlies has made it out."

"We'll go," I say. Julie glares at me when I say it. She absolutely *hates* dolls.

"You know that things always go wrong when people split up in scary movies?" Tanesha asks.

"Yes, but if we all go floor by floor it will take forever. Who knows what will have happened to the others by then?"

Everyone seems to see the logic in my rationale, even though it *does* feel safer in one large group. And it definitely feels safer in the hall. Nothing strange is going on here. So far. There's even a large plastic cauldron of candy sitting by the door, and some individual packs of apple juice. At least we won't starve.

"Okay, then," I say. "We meet back here in an hour, got it? Stay in your groups. We don't want anyone else getting lost."

Patricia and Ed both nod.

"Let's go," Patricia says.

"One hour," Ed replies.

I don't mention that my watch doesn't seem to be working. I don't want to freak them out.

Hopefully, we'll all be back here in just a few minutes.

Hopefully, this will all be over soon.

Whatever it is.

It's a lot of things to hope for, and I have a sick feeling in my gut that says none of them will happen.

# 33

**We stand outside the door to the haunted toy factory.**
Tanesha waits coolly by my side, and Julie hovers
behind us. Patricia and Maribeth have already gone
upstairs to find Lily, and I know Ed and James are
downstairs, searching for their lost teammate in the
fun house.

Even though it's just a door—plain wood, no
decorations—I'm intimidated to open it. I don't want
to even put my hand on the doorknob. I feel like I can
hear the door breathing. As if it's expectant. Waiting
for us to come inside.

As if it's excited for our terror.

"Ready, Banshees?" I ask. My voice shakes a little, but I don't think the others care. We're all scared. None of this should be happening. But it is. We have to do this. It's the only logical way forward.

My friends nod.

"If it gets too dangerous," I continue, "we leave immediately. And no matter what, we need to stay together. We can't let anyone get left behind."

I place my hand on the doorknob.

The door opens inward before I even turn it.

Like I said . . . waiting for us.

The three of us step in. Julie holds a flashlight in her hands, the beam shaking in the darkness. And that's all there is. The door clicks shut behind us, and all we see is darkness.

"This can't be right," I whisper.

Something clangs to the floor in front of us in response. We back up.

And keep going.

"Guys," Julie whispers. "The *door*."

I don't have to ask what she's talking about.

I reach behind us in the inky blackness and know for myself, just as the lights in the factory flicker on and reveal the nightmare we have landed in.

The door is gone.

# 34

**This isn't like any factory I've seen before.**

Metal ducts snake across the ceiling, and harsh light flickers from overhead metal grates. Giant pieces of boxlike machinery tower around us, blinking with lights and codes, all of them connected by silent conveyor belts.

I want to say the factory is empty, but it's not.

Because at every single station is a mannequin in denim coveralls. And on the conveyor belts, in every stage of production, are empty toy boxes.

Everything is still and silent.

And waiting.

"I don't want to be here," Julie says. Her voice wavers.

"I don't either," I reply. Because before, when I would go into a haunted house, I knew everything we saw was just a trick. Something created by a normal human like me to scare people. But now I'm positive that's not the case.

This place doesn't just want to scare us.

It wants to keep us here. Forever.

Here, every single scare and danger is real.

"Come on," Tanesha says. She steps past me, toward the warren of aisles. "We have to start somewhere. Might as well be here and now."

I swallow.

"Do we call out their names?" I ask.

She looks at me, but she doesn't answer. Even our quiet voices echo loudly in the factory. Like there's no one else alive.

Immediately, I fear the worst. What if something's already happened to the missing kids? What if they've been turned into dolls or packed up tight or a hundred other terrible scenarios?

Tanesha seems to follow my train of thought. She

starts calling out the kids' names. I flinch at the first holler of her voice. It's loud. Too loud. But when only silence responds, I start calling out as well.

Together, the three of us slowly make our way into the depths of the toy factory. There's no point trying to remember which way we came from, not when there's no door back. Still, I keep glancing behind me as we trek down the main aisle. I really wish we had string or breadcrumbs; we're no good to the missing kids if we can't find a way out.

Giant machines rise up on either side of us, all blinking lights and shiny metal, our terrified faces staring back. Our real fear, however, comes from the mannequin workers. They linger everywhere, arms upraised as if pulling levers or sorting toys. Frozen. Their blank faces are smooth as bowls, but for some reason, that makes them even scarier.

Everything is silent. Absolutely silent. Save for our infrequent calls out to the missing team. Farther in we go. And as the heavy quiet settles on our shoulders and the mannequin workers crowd around us, those calls grow quieter and quieter, until even Tanesha is barely whispering.

"I don't like this," I finally say. "Why don't we hear anyone?"

The graveyard had been *alive*. Haunted. Filled with wind and mist and lightning and zombies. I had expected a dozen toy monsters to leap out at us by now. For this to be a nightmare. Instead, there's just that sense that the factory is quietly waiting for us. And I don't want to find out what it will do once it stops waiting.

"Maybe we should go back," Tanesha says. She looks behind us. "Connect with the rest of the group. We can all come through and comb the factory together."

"Maybe you're right," I say. I call out for the missing kids one more time. I don't expect a response.

But then I hear something, coming from our left.

*"Help!"*

It's so faint, at first I think it's my imagination. Except Tanesha's eyes are wide as she stares in the direction of the voice.

"That's them!" I say.

"It could be a trap," Julie warns.

We have no other choice. We have to go on.

We start walking toward the voice, but the mannequins here are closer together, and even though I try my best to slip between them, I hit one with my shoulder.

It wobbles.

I reach out, try to steady it, but my hands are too slick from fear, and it slips from my grasp and falls.

It feels like slow motion, watching it fall over. When it hits the ground and explodes into a dozen pieces, however, time speeds back up. The crash echoes down the long corridor.

One by one, the other mannequins snap

their heads

to attention.

# 35

For a moment, the three of us stand there, and it's like everything is frozen. The mannequins stare at us blankly. We stare back.

And then,
    with the click and roar of machinery,
    the entire factory
        comes
            to
                life.
    Gears spin,
  lights strobe,
    conveyor belts rotate,

and the mannequins
    start
        moving.
Their limbs are jerky, like marionettes. A few stay
at their stations, pulling levers or sorting dolls, but
the rest
    —far too many—
begin walking
    toward
        us.
They clog the aisle we just walked down.
                            *No way to get through.*
The only way out is into the unknown.
                    Toward the voice of the missing kid.
"RUN!" I yell.
    I don't have to tell the others twice.
We dart away, dodging mannequins that swing
their arms blindly. Tanesha cuts down a side passage,
and we follow hastily. It's narrow and steam and pipes
twist every which way, but we duck and run and try to
find our way through the flashing lights and fog. My
breath is hot in my throat and Tanesha and Julie pant

at my side over the harsh roar and hiss of the machinery. The passage widens ahead of us, and I hear someone yelling out. Behind us, mannequins crowd through the passage, pushing past and over one another as they reach out with their cold plastic hands . . .

*They're gaining on us.*

Panicked, we burst out into another wide room. More machines and conveyor belts wall us in, but there aren't any mannequins in here. Just rows and rows of toy boxes. I stare around, trying to figure out the exit.

Boxes tumble behind me and I yelp.

Tanesha is toppling boxes over the passageway's entrance, forming a large pile.

"That won't hold them for long," she says as she stares up at the mound of boxes. Behind them, we can hear the mannequins thumping against the cardboard. The boxes jolt with every thud.

"We have to get out of here," I say. "Do you see—"

"There!" Julie yells. I turn and follow her pointing finger.

High on a stalled conveyor belt are three large boxes, bigger than I am tall. Plastic front and cardboard back, the type you'd find a doll or action figure in.

Except these aren't holding toys.

They're holding kids.

Matthew—the leader of the Creepy Crawlies—bangs on the plastic and calls out for help the moment he sees us. His voice is muffled through the plastic.

"We have to help them," Julie says.

I nod. "You two keep the mannequins at bay. I'll go grab him."

The conveyor belt the box is on stretches between two giant machines, easily two stories off the ground. Just looking at it gives me vertigo. But while Tanesha and Julie press themselves to the pile of boxes, I run toward one of the machines and start climbing, clambering up boxes and grabbing on to gears. Everything is chaos—Julie and Tanesha yelling out in frustration, the kids in the boxes calling for help, the thudding of mannequin fists, and the distant grind of machinery.

My foot slips on a box, and the pile I've been

standing on crumbles out from under me. I grab on to
a pipe and hold on for dear life.

The pipe

slowly

pulls

d
o
w
n.


I look up in fear; it's not a pipe after all, but a
lever! And the moment it clicks into place, the machine
I was climbing purrs into motion. Lights flash and a
siren wails, and behind me, there's a crash of boxes
hitting the ground as a mannequin arm breaks
through. My heart thuds painfully in my throat as I
struggle to get a foothold. When I look up again,
shock pulses through me.

The conveyor belt is moving, pulling the Creepy Crawlies toward the second machine.

And judging from the grinding noise in that other machine, I don't want them to reach the end of it.

I gather all my strength and climb the rest of the way up the machine, then wobble my way out across the moving conveyor belt. It groans and rattles and pulls beneath my feet. I try not to look down.

But I can't help it.

I do.

My vision sways.

I'm so high up.

*I hate heights.*

Almost as much as Julie hates dolls.

For a moment, I think I'm going to faint. Until I hear the kids thudding on the walls of their boxes again, and I remember that I am needed. There's no time for weakness or fear.

I run over to the nearest box and rip open the tape holding it shut. The side opens and Matthew collapses in front of me, gasping for air.

"Thank you," he says.

I reach down and help him up.

"Don't thank me yet," I say when he stands. "We still have to get out of here."

Below us, Julie and Tanesha shriek and run as the entire pyramid of fallen boxes explodes away, and the mannequins that were chasing us stumble into the room.

# 36

Hurriedly, Matthew and I release his two teammates from their cardboard prisons. We leap onto a pile of boxes and slide down to the floor. Tanesha and Julie stand there, watching the mannequins spill in with terrified expressions on their zombie faces.

"What are we going to do?" Julie yells.

"It's the machines!" Matthew replies. "If we can turn them off, the mannequins will stop."

I don't ask if he's sure, because there's no time—we're trapped, and this is our only chance.

"Quick! Find an off button!"

We run to machines and press buttons and pull levers. My pulse races.

This isn't going to work.

Behind us, the mannequins stagger closer, reaching out. Tanesha yells and swats at one that grabs her hair; the mannequin falls back to the ground and shatters.

One near me grabs my arm. I try to fight it off, but it's strong, too strong, and when it pulls me around to face it my vision shifts, and it's not a mannequin in a worker's uniform facing me, but the faceless bride.

"*You did this,*" she hisses, her grip cold as ice and strong as iron. The rest of the factory fades away, until it is just her and me in the darkness. "*This is your fault. For what you have done, I will keep you here forever!*"

I try to fight her off, but she's strong, so strong—

"Got it!" Julie yells.

And just like that, the mannequin is just a mannequin in coveralls again. The machines around us whir to a halt. The floor is crowded with mannequin workers, at least a hundred. But they've stopped. They've all stopped.

I wrench myself free from the frozen mannequin's grasp and, trembling, make my way over to the group.

"Let's get out of here," I say. My voice shakes. What was that vision? What did she mean, this was all my fault?

And was she telling the truth? What if we truly *can't* escape?

# 37

**We navigate our way through the aisles of the factory.**
Now that the mannequins are all turned off, the halls
are actually somewhat empty. Matthew asks us
what's going on, but when it becomes clear that no
one really has a clue, we all fall into silence.

Some rescue mission this is.

"I don't get it," Tanesha says after a while. Our
feet echo down the aisle, and her voice seems far too
loud in the silence. "This is a toy factory, right?" She
looks at Matthew when she says it, as if he is in charge
of how it all turned out.

Matthew nods.

"So we've seen mannequin workers and empty boxes, but where are all the toys?"

"There were loads earlier," Megan—one of the Creepy Crawlies—says. "That's how we were captured. I was putting up a display of possessed teddy bears when they actually came alive and attacked. The toys dragged us away and put us into those boxes."

I swallow hard and look down a passing side aisle. Light flickers at the end, and the shadows on the floor move.

"So where are they now?" Julie asks.

"Let's not find out," I say. "We need to worry about finding the exit."

"If there *is* an exit," Julie whispers, so quiet I barely hear it.

We round a corner, and there, at the far end of a dark hall, is a blinking red sign with one unmistakable word: **EXIT**.

Matthew whoops in excitement and runs ahead of us.

I call out his name. Yell at him to stop.

He trips.

Lights flicker on.

We've found the missing toys.

# 38

Every single surface in the wide-open room is covered with toys. And these aren't the cute toys you'd see at a store either. The dolls are missing heads and arms, and the teddy bears have vicious fangs, and the action figures all look like monstrous mutants. Even though they're all shorter than my knee, I still flinch back at the sight of them.

There are hundreds.

*Thousands.*

And they're all looking at us.

"What do we do?" Tanesha asks.

The exit sign flickers on the other side of the

room, but the only way to get there is through the toys. Even though they're still right now, I have no doubt that the moment we step in there, they're going to attack.

My mind races.

Once more, machines line every wall, and conveyor belts stretch overhead. If we could make it up there, we could maybe sneak our way across. The trouble is, the nearest ladder is twenty feet away, and I'd have to wade through the toys to get there.

I take a step forward.

As one, all the toys in the room step toward me. Just one step, but their feet thud like thunder.

I freeze. The toys freeze as well.

I take a step back.

The toys take a step back.

"They're mirroring us," I whisper, and I hope I'm telling the truth.

I step to my left.

Sure enough, the toys follow suit. They might just be mirroring us now, but I have no doubt that if we were to step fully into that room, they'd rip us apart.

"How are we going to get past them?" Julie asks. Tears build at the corners of her eyes.

"We need a distraction," Tanesha says. She looks around, but there's nothing in the room except us and the toys.

That's when things click. I gesture to the boxlike machine beside us. It's about six feet tall, and we can totally reach the top if we help each other. There's nothing nearby, but at least it gets us off the floor.

"Everybody up!" I say. "Quickly."

They do so, hoisting each other up until they're all safe and sound atop the machine. All of them except me.

"Stay here," I say to them. "I'll be right back."

Then I take off down the hall behind us, heading to do what I'm positive is a very bad idea.

# 39

I've done a lot of stupid stuff in my life, but as I run away from a horde of mechanized mannequins I intentionally reanimated, I know without a doubt that this is the worst.

Their feet echo like gunshots on the concrete floor behind me. I don't look back. My breath burns and my legs want to give out—I've never been the most athletic kid—but I keep running. Down the long aisle leading toward my friends. Toward the exit.

Toward the horde of toys that I know will tear us apart if we don't distract them.

I reach the exit chamber and veer toward the

machine my friends were safely on. It isn't there! It's farther into the room, right in the middle of the toys, and it's then that I realize my mistake: The machine is on tracks, and it's heading straight for the exit. When I pulled the lever to make the mannequins come alive, I must have triggered the motion on the machine. It slowly inches its way toward the exit door, bringing my friends and the Creepy Crawlies to safety . . . and farther away from me.

I panic.

There's nowhere to hide or climb, and the moment I run into the room, the dolls and teddy bears and action figures spring to life.

They swarm toward me in a tide of tiny plastic hands and sharp teeth.

The dolls cry out my name in creepy baby voices, their blank glass eyes trained on me.

The teddy bears growl loudly as their claws extend from tiny furry paws.

I try to back up, but the mannequins are right behind me.

"Kevin!" my friends call out. But it's too late.

Tiny, cold plastic arms wrap around my chest.

I yell out as the dolls grab me. Yell out as my friends reach the safety of the exit. I know I should feel happy, because they got away. They're going to be safe. Wasn't that the plan all along?

But as the dolls drag me to my knees and the toys swarm me, all I can think is that this is the most scared I've been in my entire life.

# 40

Darkness surrounds me.

Heavy, cold darkness, quiet as grave dirt.

Am I dead?

Is this what it feels like to be buried alive?

But no. My legs are sore and I'm thirsty and when I strain my ears I can hear something. Music.

Wait, is it . . . carnival music?

Instantly, I realize my mistake.

I'm not dead.

I'm not buried.

I've been taken to the next part of the haunted house.

The music gets louder, and it sounds like the sort of pipe organ waltz you'd hear on a merry-go-round. And as the music amplifies, lights flicker on above me. Long strings of white globes, the ceiling above them draped in red-and-black-striped fabric.

A circus tent.

I'm in the middle of a circus tent, in the middle of a great dirt ring.

The light and the music grow, revealing rows of bleachers circling me.

They aren't empty.

Mannequins line every bench, all of them dressed in normal clothes—jeans and T-shirts and sweaters—and all of them posed as if waiting for me to do a trick. I look around. There's no one and nothing else in the center ring with me, and the bleachers circle the entire stage. Except for one aisle to my right.

For a long time, I don't move. I just stand there and listen to the carnival music and watch the crowd watch me. I wait for a mannequin to move. For toys to break in and grab me. But nothing happens. The mannequins are waiting. I take a step toward the aisle; with the thud of boots, two burly mannequins dressed as clowns step out from the shadows. Blocking the exit.

I take a step back into the ring, and a spotlight blinks on and nearly blinds me. The music swells to a roar; I realize the mannequins aren't just posing.

They are watching me.

Waiting for me.

To do what?

I feel like I'm supposed to be putting on a show. Maybe that's it? Maybe I'm supposed to perform, and when my act is done, I can leave? The question is, what can I possibly perform? All I'm good at is putting together haunted houses.

Maybe a joke will work?

"What's a vampire's favorite circus act?" I ask the audience.

Unsurprisingly, there's no response.

"They always go for the juggler!" I yell out. I make sure to fake laugh at the end, too. "Get it? Juggler? Jugular?"

I sigh heavily. The audience doesn't move. Jokes clearly aren't the way forward.

"I can do a cartwheel?" I say. Again, no response,

but it's better than the mannequins attacking me, I guess. I ready myself and do a cartwheel.

Nothing happens. I just feel a little dizzy.

"What am I supposed to do?"

I stare around at the silent mannequins. Frustration builds. I feel like a fool, but there doesn't seem to be any way out. There's no way I want to try taking on the guards. Which means there's only one more trick up my sleeve. It's not a very good one at that.

Bobbing my head in time to the circus music, I close my eyes and start to dance.

I'm *not* a good dancer. I don't know what I'm doing. I bounce up and down on my heels, nodding my head. When that doesn't seem to be enough, I start hopping around from foot to foot, spinning and throwing my hands up in the air. I even throw in a dab or two for good measure. I feel like a fool. The lack of applause isn't helping.

I don't know how long I dance in the spotlight. I keep my eyes squeezed shut and spin around in circles and hope against hope that this will be enough to get me out of here.

Someone starts clapping.

I stop immediately and open my eyes.

Patricia stands in the aisle, shaking her head and watching me with a smile on her face.

"What in the *world* are you doing?" she asks.

"What are you doing here?" I reply. I feel the blush rising to my cheeks. I can't believe she of all people saw that.

"Looking for stragglers," she says. She drops her hands, and the smile slips, too. "Actually, I'm . . . lost."

"Lost? How did you get in here?"

"I was in the attic and couldn't find my way out of the labyrinth. I was running away from a really scary Minotaur when I fell down a hole. I must have blacked out, because the next thing I knew, I was here."

"The others?"

"I managed to find Lily. She and Maribeth got out. What about you?"

"Same. We found the Creepy Crawlies and they got out with the rest of my team, but I was taken by the dolls."

"Dolls?" Patricia asks. She shudders. "Now *that's* creepy."

"How did you get past the guards?" I ask.

I step closer to her, fully expecting the manne-quins in the stands to rise and attack. They stay seated. Maybe I'm a better dancer than I thought?

"What guards?" she asks. "I saw a tent and heard music and came in to see you dancing like a fool."

Again, the blush rises in my cheeks, but when she smiles at me this time, it isn't quite so mean.

"Come on," I say. "Let's find the exit. It has to be here somewhere."

She nods.

As I brush past her, something in the audience catches my eye. I pause and look back. But no, I must have been imagining it.

I thought it was the mannequin bride.

# 41

I don't know what I expect to see when we leave the circus tent. But I know it's not the long, twisting corridor of striped fabric that stretches out before us. I blink. I have to be seeing things.

"Is that going upside down?" I whisper.

The hall seems to spiral, so that farther down, the ceiling is actually the floor. Just looking at it makes my head hurt and spin.

"This wasn't here when I arrived," Patricia says. She swallows hard and looks at me. "The door led me straight to the tent. This . . ."

"This is a fun house," I finish. I square my shoulders. "It's not going to make getting out easy. But if this is like a real one, everything is just an illusion. I hope."

I start walking forward, and Patricia follows at my side. The hall spirals with every step and my stomach rises to my throat, but I refuse to throw up with Patricia right there. I have to look strong and assured.

Though . . . when I glance over at her, she doesn't look like her usual self. She doesn't seem ready to insult or taunt.

I only look at her for a moment. Even that glance is enough to make my head spin from vertigo—from the corner of my eye, the arch to the circus tent we just left appears to be sideways.

"What if we don't make it out of here?" Patricia asks.

Her voice is quiet, sucked up by the vinyl walls of the corridor.

"We will," I say. "It's just a maze. They always have an exit."

"Not the fun house," she replies. "But the mansion. We tried *everything*, Kevin. What if . . ."

"There's no point worrying about something like

that," I say. "We just have to take this one thing at a time. First, we get out of here. Then we worry about the rest."

"I don't know how you can be so calm about all of this."

The truth is, I'm not. Maybe I'm good at hiding it, but inside, I'm terrified. For a moment, I consider lying. Telling her I'm not scared at all. After all, she's done nothing but insult me and sabotage me for the last few years. But that doesn't seem right. For the first time since I've known her, she isn't being mean to me. That makes me want to be kind and honest in return.

"Honestly? I'm more scared than I've ever been." My words are quiet but assured. "But I have to think logically, otherwise I know I won't be able to get out of here."

"You've always been logical," Patricia says. "That's why I've always been intimidated by you."

I pause.

"You? You were intimidated by me?"

She nods but keeps looking straight ahead.

"Last year, the night before we opened, I . . . I

went and looked at your room. Your laboratory was amazing. It looked like a real lab—you had everything thought out perfectly, from the moment you stepped in the door to the moment you left. Even when it was empty and turned off, it was brilliant. I had just put together a bunch of things that I thought were scary, but you . . . you had thought everything through. Logical. You made it a story. You truly knew horror, and you knew how to make it work for you. And *I* knew in that moment that I didn't have a chance at beating you."

She hangs her head.

"At least, not fairly."

I swallow hard. There's a part of me that glows with her praise. The rest of me is hot with anger over what she did because she was intimidated.

I'll never forget it.

Coming in opening night, everything looking just fine. I had been dressed as an evil scientist, and Julie and Tanesha were my subjects. In theory, it should have been terrifying—Tanesha was going to have rubber tentacles writhing from her chest, and Julie was getting sawed in half by a robot. And then, the moment the judges started going through, the entire showcase malfunctioned. Glitter began spraying out of the bubbling test tubes. Pop music blared from the speakers that should have been playing creepy lab noises. And then, from the ceiling, a bunch of pink feathers and confetti exploded, making the entire scene look like some really strange music video rather than a creepy montage. She'd even found a way to make the wriggling tentacles dance in time to the music.

"You could have just lost," I say, the memory sour in my chest. "You didn't have to cheat."

"I did, though," she replies. She glances at me, and the corners of her eyes fill with tears. "My parents are super strict at home, and this was the one time I got to do something fun. I knew if I lost that they wouldn't let me do it again. They'd say it was a waste of time. So I cheated. Because it was the only way I could keep doing what I loved."

"I didn't know," I say. "I didn't know it meant so much to you. Like it does to me."

"Yeah, well . . ."

"You didn't have to be mean to me," I say. "All

this year. You could have been nice. We could have been teammates."

She looks at me again, and her smile is sad. "My parents would never allow that. They'd say I was giving up. Or that I was using you to win. I didn't want to be mean to you. It was just easier than admitting I was scared that you were better."

I don't know why I do it. She's been so horrible, and for the last year I've viewed her as my biggest enemy. But for some unknown reason, in that twisted, creepy hallway, I reach out and take her hand. As friends.

"We'll get out of here," I say. "And that will make us all winners." I almost want to tell her about my own rule breaking in the pursuit of winning. Almost.

She smiles and opens her mouth, but her words are cut short.

Because that's when the clowns leap in.

# 42

Patricia screams as a half dozen clown mannequins in poufy striped outfits bounce and cartwheel in through a flap in the curtain walls. They encircle her, laughing and howling, their makeup terrifying— enormous red mouths and bone-white faces.

And no eyes.

I scream as they swarm past me in a flurry of bells and giggles, knocking Patricia's hand from mine and pushing me to the ground. But they aren't interested in me.

In only a matter of moments, they pick Patricia up

and carry her back through the wall, leaving just me and a ringing, echoing silence.

I'm frozen in place. Unable to stand or run after her. I stare at the space she just occupied, my head spinning. Did that really just happen?

Shock fades, replaced by a jolt of adrenaline. I jump to my wobbly feet and rush toward the break in the wall.

When I push aside the flap, the only thing facing me is concrete.

# 43

**I don't know what to do.**

Patricia was taken before my very eyes, and the exit she was dragged through isn't an exit at all. Just another wall.

I pound at it, but it isn't hollow. I graze my hands over the surface, but there aren't any hidden buttons or switches. The wall isn't an illusion or trick. Patricia isn't hiding behind a screen. Whatever those clowns did, they took her for real. And that means I have to find her. Before they hurt her for real.

I look toward the flickering darkness at the far end of the hall, the great unknown. Dread settles over me. Anything could happen in here. Anything could be waiting.

That also means that anything could be happening to Patricia, and I'm the only one who can stop it.

With a very frail sort of bravery, I clench my fists and stalk forward, into the darkness. I'm not prepared for anything, but I don't have a choice. I have to face it.

I expect the hallway to go on forever, continually spiraling in on itself until I go sick with vertigo. But after only a few dozen steps into the flickering shadows, red string lights blink on, revealing a wooden door with a big bronze knob.

Something is scratched into the door. At first, I think they're weird symbols. Then I realize they're words, written in a very creepy handwriting. As if scratched in by talons.

### BEWARE:
### WITHIN LURKS
### THE MOST TERRIFYING CREATURE
### IN EXISTENCE

I gulp. That can't be good.

What sort of horrors could a fun house hold?

Maybe it's a sideshow of oddities, like the Fiji Mermaid or two-headed snake?

Maybe it holds cages of monstrous lions with slavering, poisonous fangs?

My brain races with every horror movie I've seen, every monster that has haunted my nightmares.

I can't even imagine which one is the most terrifying of them all. I can't imagine which will be locked inside. I've never been scared of monsters before. But I've also never had to face a real one. Alone.

I place my hand on the doorknob. The door rattles at my touch, banging against the hinges. I yelp and take a step back. For a moment, I consider turning around and running away.

Maybe there was another exit in the circus tent.

Maybe if I did a good enough trick they'd let us all go.

Maybe I don't have to face the monster at all.

Maybe . . .

"You have to do this," I say aloud to myself. "You

*can* do this. You can do anything. Nothing scares you."

The last one sounds like a lie, but I put my hand on the door anyway.

Even though I hear roaring from the other side, even though it rattles as if some monstrous beast is clawing to get out, I slowly turn the brass doorknob. I squeeze my eyes shut.

And when the door opens, I don't even look.

I take a deep breath and leap inside.

# 44

I expect to feel claws on my skin or hot breath on my neck, but as I stand there with my eyes closed and wince against the loud growling, I feel nothing but a chill breeze. Light flickers behind my eyes. I open them, and a wave of relief floods through me.

An old-fashioned gramophone sits beside the door, playing a record of beast noises on loop. Meanwhile, a mechanical lever attached to the door frame shakes it wildly.

Tricks. Just tricks.

I turn and face the rest of the room and am dazzled by the display.

Mirrors are everywhere. It's a labyrinth of mirrors, some so tall I can't see the top, others barely higher than my knee. Some are flat and others are distorted, and when I look at them a thousand versions of myself stare back. I actually let out a laugh.

The scariest creature in the world is just . . . me?

A very good trick. I may have to use that next year.

Patricia's distant scream shakes me from my momentary musing. I'm still stuck in a truly haunted house. I still have to find her and escape. Planning next year's fright can wait.

Squaring my shoulders, I head toward the maze of mirrors. If the only scary thing in here is myself, I'll have no problem facing it. After all, I see myself every day . . . right?

The first hall of mirrors makes me pause and giggle. My reflections laugh back with me—in one mirror I'm two feet shorter, in the next I'm double my height. The next makes me narrower, the next wider. I keep walking, watching my shape change before my eyes. My skin turns pink and purple and green. My ears grow and shrink along with my nose and eyes. In one, I look like a mouse; in another, an elephant.

In the next, my face is so squinched up I barely have any features at all.

This isn't scary! I wish the others could be here, seeing this.

And just like that, when I reach the next mirror, I'm not alone in it at all. Tanesha stands beside me, and Julie on my other side. Except their expressions wipe the smile from my face.

They both look angry. They look angry at *me*.

I keep walking.

In the next mirror, I'm back down in the basement. It's like watching TV. It's no longer a real graveyard, but our created scene. I watch as Tanesha confronts me. I can't hear any words, but I remember them well. This isn't an illusion at all—this is what really happened. This is when she learned I had stolen the mannequin and hidden it away. Except now, I can't look away from the disappointed expression she wears.

In the next mirror, I watch the judges warily walk through our display. Julie and Tanesha both play amazing zombies, and I guide the judges past the swamp with its flickering lights and smoke, through the willow trees, and up to the final scare: the gazebo. I step to the side and gesture them forward. When they walk up to it, the ghostly mannequin swings out with flashing lights. One of the judges leaps high in the air. The other silently screams. Then they all laugh nervously. Clearly, this scare was the best they'd experienced.

My heart thrills. Maybe this is my fortune. Maybe this room is just proving that we *will* get out of this and we *will* win.

But then I move on to the next mirror.

I hold the trophy for best haunted room. Except Tanesha and Julie aren't at my side; they're walking away, heads down. Everyone else around me is applauding for a job well done.

Clearly, though, the victory is lost on my friends.

In the next mirror, Tanesha and Julie confront me. I see them mouth the words *cheater* and *liar* and *mannequin* and my heart drops. But my reflection just stands there defiantly, yelling back silently that they are jealous.

*No, no, don't be mean to them!* I want to yell out, but it's just a mirror, just a reflection.

I leave this mirror and move on, but the next isn't any better. I'm alone in my room. All the photos I used to have of Julie and Tanesha are torn down. I sit on my bed and stare at my phone, but I can see there aren't any messages. When I scroll through my contacts, they aren't even listed. I know then that they've abandoned me. For cheating at the haunted house. For lying about the mannequin. For putting everyone in danger.

*Yes*, I hear in my brain. *You are the reason they were in danger. This is your fault.*

I move on to the next. As I go, I catch sight of someone else in the bedroom with me.

A woman in white . . .

This mirror isn't a mirror at all.

It's a window.

A window looking down at my trapped friends and the other teams.

They huddle in the hall of the mansion and pound at the door to get out. A few of them are crying. Shadows creep down the walls and I know that the horrors are no longer confined to their rooms.

The nightmares are leaching out.

Taking over.

Soon, not even the hallway will be safe, and my friends will be lost forever.

"No," I whisper, watching them. "I have to help them. I have to—"

I blink, and I'm no longer in a hall of mirrors.

I'm back in the middle of the circus tent. Only now there aren't any mannequins in the bleachers. There isn't any creepy circus music.

Just me and two full-length mirrors in the center ring.

Just me, and a terrible choice.

# 45

There's no doubt in my mind now why the door said that the mirror room contained the most terrifying monster out there.

Because when I think of what I've done to get here, what I've done by inadvertently cursing this entire house, I know that I'm the true monster. I let my ego get the better of me by lying to my friends and abusing the memory of some poor, dead girl. All she wanted was to be left in peace, but I had to put her on display. The mannequin bride might be the one who cast the curse over the house and turned the attractions real, but I know with every bit of me that I'm the real monster in here. I feel horrible. And as I stare at the two mirrors in front of me, that terrible clenching in my gut only worsens.

One mirror still shows the hallway, my friends and teammates huddled against the door as the shadows reach in. The only person missing is Patricia. In that mirror, a shadow of myself appears and steps past them. My ghostly hand touches the door, and when it does so the door swings open, and outside the house all of our parents reach out to hug us. I know that if I walk through this mirror, this will be the outcome: We get to leave. We get to put this terrible experience behind us.

All of us escape.

Except for Patricia.

When I glance at the other mirror I see her there, in the gazebo on the hill, the ghostly bride mannequin bearing down on her. I know that if I walk through this mirror I will have to face the mannequin. I will have to try to save Patricia, and there's a very good chance I will fail. There's a very good chance we will all be trapped here forever.

These are my choices: Save my friends and let my

enemy suffer, or risk everything to save the girl who—
only a few days ago—would have gladly left me
behind.

I swallow. It shouldn't be a hard choice, but it is,
and that tells me that I truly am the monster. It tells
me that there truly is only one choice to make.

I close my eyes and step through the mirror.

# 46

"Kevin!" her voice rings out. "What are you doing here?"

"Saving you," I reply.

Patricia cowers against the banister of the gazebo. All around us the croaking of frogs and rumbles of thunder echo through the heavy fog. Other noises, too, permeate the dark: the moans of zombies, the crunch of opening coffins, the wails of ghosts. Chills race down my spine, but the sounds are nothing compared to the fear from what stands before me and Patricia. The monster that brought all of this about.

Well, the monster other than myself.

The ghostly bride hovers in the air, her tattered wedding dress billowing in the breeze, her veil hiding a shadowed nothingness of a face. Just seeing her makes me want to cower in fear. Not just because she is terrifying, but because I know I am the one who made her.

"You have cursed your friends with your greed," the bride says. "Why did you do it? Why couldn't you let me rest?"

Patricia latches on to my arm and stares at the ghostly bride.

"What is she talking about, Kevin?" Patricia asks. "Why is she acting like it's your fault?"

"Because it is," I reply. I take a deep breath and step forward, putting myself in between Patricia and the ghost. "I wanted to win more than anything. Even if it meant stealing. I broke a mannequin in the basement, and when Mr. Evans hid it away, I snuck behind everyone's back and stole it to use as a prop. I'm the reason the ghost got angry. I'm the reason all of this went bad."

"And you will rot here forever because of it," the ghost bride says. "It was bad enough that my parents wouldn't let me rest. Bad enough that I had to remain on display for them. I had hoped, when they passed, that I, too, would be able to move on. But I was stuck in that mannequin. Trapped away forever. At least, for a time, I was in darkness. And then you broke me, decided to use me as a prop. You forced me back. Forced me to be another *attraction*. Now I am stuck forever. All I want is to move on. To be with my love."

"I'm sorry, Anna," I say to the ghost. "I really am. I didn't mean for any of this to happen. I just . . . I wanted to win so badly, I was willing to do whatever it took." I glance back at Patricia, but it's not in anger. In that moment, we are very much the same, and I can tell from her expression that she is just as sorry for last year's sabotage as I am for this. I look back to the bride. "I'm sorry you were hurt. And I'm sorry you weren't able to move on. I should never have used your life story as a prop. It wasn't right."

"Touching words," the ghost says. Am I imagining it, or is she crying? "But regret will not get you out of here."

"I know," I say. I swallow the fear in my throat

and take another, shaky step forward. "That's why I propose a deal."

"A deal?"

"To make up for what I've done. *I'm* the one who did this. *I'm* the one who broke the mannequin and put you on display. You should punish me, and only me. Let my friends go and I'll stay here, with you, forever."

Silence echoes around us, so deep not even the thunder or frogs ring through.

"You would stay here?" the mannequin asks. "You would willingly sacrifice yourself to save your friends? And your enemy?"

I reach back and take Patricia's hand.

"She's not an enemy. She's a friend. And yes, if it means saving them, I would stay here with you. I'm the one you want to punish. Not them. Let them go. Let's end this so you can be in peace."

"A selfless act," the bride whispers. "So be it."

I barely have time to blink. One moment she hovers a few feet away.

The next, she is on me, her hands gripping my

shoulders and her veiled face only inches from mine. For a moment, I see my own face shadowed in the depths of her veil, my own greed and pride reflected back.

Then the ghost bride screams, and everything around me goes dark.

# 47

"Kevin! Kevin, are you okay?" Julie's voice rouses me from the darkness. It feels like swimming up through gelatin, but my eyes finally open to see a faint stream of light.

"What . . . ?" I whisper.

We're outside, on the manor's porch. Adults and kids in costume swarm around us, and a fire truck sits at the curb with its lights silently spinning.

"We did it," Julie says. "We got out."

"All of us?" I ask.

"All of us," Patricia replies. She kneels down beside me.

"But how am I . . . I thought I . . ."

She puts her hand on my shoulder and smiles knowingly. "You did a selfless thing, offering to sacrifice yourself to save me. I guess that must have been enough to appease the ghost and get us all out. Maybe someone doing a selfless act was enough to put her soul at peace."

Timid hope blooms in my chest. I push myself to sitting, and then Tanesha helps me stand.

"I don't know what you did," Tanesha says, "but you did it. We're free."

Julie smiles excitedly. "And! The adults decided that we all win this year, and everyone gets free pizza."

"They think we got accidentally locked inside," Tanesha explains. "They feel bad for scaring us like that. But they don't know what *really* happened."

"Why didn't you tell them?" I ask.

She shrugs. "Who would believe us? I sure wouldn't. I mean, everything inside is back to normal. If you want to look."

I eagerly shake my head no.

"I think I'm good on haunted houses for a while."

Tanesha and Julie burst into laughter, and Patricia and I quickly follow. I see my dads through the crowd. They walk toward me, concern clear on their faces.

"I should probably go say hi," I say, nodding to my parents. My friends nod, but Patricia stops me before I walk away.

"Thank you," she says. "For what you did. For saving me. I'm . . . I'm really sorry about everything I've put you through. If it means anything, I've always thought you were the best at what you do."

I smile. "Thank you," I reply. "That means a lot. And I've always thought you were pretty great, too."

"Maybe next year we can all work together?" Patricia suggests. "I bet we could make something *truly* terrifying."

I chuckle. "You want to make another haunted house? After what just happened?"

She grins. "It should be fine. Just so long as neither of us tries to cheat again."

"Deal," I say. We shake hands.

"Kevin!" Poppa Jared calls. "We're so happy you're all right."

I give Patricia a quick hug and then jog through the crowd of parents toward my dads. They wrap me in a big bear hug.

"What happened in there?" Poppa Blake asks.

They each take one of my hands and begin walking toward the truck. Everything already feels like a dream. A distant nightmare.

"You'll never believe it," I say. "Let's just say that things got a lot scarier than we expected."

"But *nothing* scares you," Poppa Jared says.

"Must have been truly scary, then," Poppa Blake finishes.

I chuckle. "You have no idea."

Now that we've escaped, the fear fades away, replaced with excitement. We made it through. We experienced something terrifying. And now I have a ton of ideas for next year. Though Patricia's right—we definitely need to make sure not to upset any ghosts this time.

We reach the truck and I hop in, casting one quick glance at the manor before I go.

And there, in the upper windows, are two mannequins staring out. One is the ghostly bride.

The other, with its hands pressed to the windows and its mouth open in a scream, looks an awful lot like me.

# Acknowledgments

Words cannot express how excited I am to be able to work on this incredible series. I grew up reading creepy stories that kept me up at night (I'm admittedly a total scaredy-cat), and it's an honor to be now writing those tales for a new generation of readers.

My deepest thanks go to David Levithan, editor extraordinaire, for being the spark that brought these books to life and the keen eye that made them truly terrifying.

To my agent, Brent Taylor of Triada Literary US, for his guidance and excitement with every new venture.

My thanks as well to Jana Haussmann and the entire Scholastic Book Fairs team for their endless support and enthusiasm. I couldn't have done any of this without them. And by "this" I mean sharing stories that have probably given a lot of readers nightmares! But in a good way, of course.

Speaking of, I want to thank you, my readers, for falling in love with these creepy little stories and sharing your excitement (and fear of dolls!) through letters and email. I've loved hearing from each and every one of you, and hope I can continue to write stories that will thrill and chill you for years to come.

# About the Author

K. R. Alexander is the pseudonym for author Alex R. Kahler.

As K. R., he writes creepy middle grade books for brave young readers. As Alex—his actual first name— he writes fantasy novels for adults and teens. In both cases, he loves writing fiction drawn from true life experiences. (But this book can't be real . . . can it?)

Alex has traveled the world collecting strange and fascinating tales, from the misty moors of Scotland to the humid jungles of Hawaii. He is always on the move, as he believes there is much more to life than what meets the eye.

You can learn more about his travels and other books, including *The Collector, The Fear Zone,* and the other books in the Scare Me series, on his website: cursedlibrary.com

He looks forward to scaring you again . . . soon.

Be afraid. Be very afraid. K. R. Alexander's latest is coming to haunt you.

## 6

**No one ever leaves Copper Hollow.**

No one really questions why. We don't have much, but everything we need is right here. Nothing is great, but nothing is terrible either. Nothing bad ever happens here. It's Copper Hollow. It's always been the same.

Some people might get bored, but not me. Not with my imagination. I can transform any situation into an adventure. I can make even a sleepy old town like Copper Hollow seem exciting. At least, that's what I tell myself. When the summer days are super long, or when I realize that this day feels exactly the same as the one before, I try to use my imagination to make everything new again. Most of the time, it works. There are times, though, when it feels like even my imagination isn't enough.

It's like a part of me is waiting for something. A *real* adventure. A real thrill.

But Copper Hollow never changes. There are no real adventures. No true thrills.

At least, not until the doll appears. Then everything changes.


Maybe I should have tried leaving Copper Hollow earlier . . . while I had a chance.